W9-BRV-118

"WHEN IT COMES TO KEEPING IT REAL, THERE IS NO ONE LIKE WENDY WILLIAMS."
—Newsweek.com

More praise for
WENDY WILLIAMS

"Williams is a real-life scandalmonger. . . . bawdy . . . commanding . . . sassily comic."

—*The New York Times*

"[Wendy's] bold personality and unvarnished opinions have made her an institution."

—*New York Daily News*

"The self-proclaimed 'Queen of All Media.'. . . Wendy is witty, quick and yes, she always has the last word. The girl spares no punches and everything is fair game. . . . rib-breaking funny."

—blackstarnews.com

"Wendy is at the top of her game."

—*Honey* magazine

This title is also available as an eBook.

Ritz Harper Goes to
HOLLYWOOD!

OTHER TITLES BY WENDY WILLIAMS

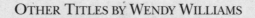

The Ritz Harper Chronicles, Book II:
Is the Bitch Dead, or What?
The Ritz Harper Chronicles, Book I:
Drama Is Her Middle Name
Wendy's Got the Heat
The Wendy Williams Experience

THE RITZ HARPER CHRONICLES, BOOK III

Ritz Harper Goes to

HOLLYWOOD!

Wendy Williams

WITH

Zondra Hughes

POCKET BOOKS

New York   London   Toronto   Sydney

Pocket Books
A Division of Simon & Schuster, Inc.
1230 Avenue of the Americas
New York, NY 10020

This book is a work of fiction. Names, characters, places,
and incidents either are products of the author's imagination or are
used fictitiously. Any resemblance to actual events or locales or
persons, living or dead, is entirely coincidental.

Copyright © 2009 by Wendy, Inc.

All rights reserved, including the right to reproduce this book
or portions thereof in any form whatsoever. For information
address Pocket Books Subsidiary Rights Department,
1230 Avenue of the Americas, New York, NY 10020

First Karen Hunter/Pocket Books trade paperback edition May 2009

POCKET and colophon are registered trademarks of
Simon & Schuster, Inc.

For information about special discounts for bulk purchases,
please contact Simon & Schuster Special Sales at
1-800-456-6798 or business@simonandschuster.com

Designed by Aline Pace

Manufactured in the United States of America

10 9 8 7 6 5 4 3 2 1

Library of Congress Cataloging-in-Publication Data is available.

ISBN-13: 978-1-4165-9288-4
ISBN-10:   1-4165-9288-1

To

Little Kev, my heart

Big Kev, my rock

And to all my fans,

without you none of this would be possible.

FROM *RITZ HARPER CHRONICLES, BOOK II:*

The last time Ritz Harper was in a hospital she was clinging to life, riddled with bullets. She didn't even visit the hospital during her aunt's last days; she hated it so much. Ritz hated the smell, she hated the nurses, she hated the whole scene. Sure, she got star treatment, the special private room with all of the amenities. But it was still a hospital.

This occasion, however, made it bearable.

Ritz was there doing something she never thought she would ever do—have a baby. She delivered in a room by herself, just as she wanted. There was only her doctor, a nurse, and an anesthesiologist. Yes, she was having an epidural. All of the pushing and hollering and that natural-childbirth shit was for the birds, she thought. *I want this baby to slide out pain-free.* But even with the epidural, Ritz swore it felt as if she were pushing an Escalade through her coochie. And she wasn't sure, but she thought she pushed so hard that she even shit on the delivery table.

All of the trauma and the pain and the embarrass-
ment were erased as with amnesia because all Ritz
could remember before she passed out was the doctor
saying, "You did great! It's a girl!"

Ritz woke up in her private room. A nurse came in,
holding a little bundle in a blanket, talking about
feeding time. Ritz had not planned on breast-feeding,
not with her implants just getting settled after one of
them had been replaced following the shooting. It was
bad enough that she had to mess up her figure for a
few months, and God knew how long it would take before she'd be back to her diva shape. She also knew
that a little nip and tuck would be in order after she
fully recovered.

"Whatever God didn't do, I know some doctor will
fix," she said to herself, knowing she would at the very
least have a tummy tuck, a butt lift, and some liposuc-
tion around her thighs.

The nurse had no expression as she handed Ritz
her baby.

"The doctor will be in in a moment to speak with
you," said the nurse solemnly before leaving the room.

Ritz looked puzzled. She held her baby and a serene sense of joy washed over her. Ritz was surprised.
She didn't know she would feel this way. Uncondi-
tional love? Was this what that felt like? Ritz realized
that she never experienced this before in her entire
life. Ritz was alone. Derek wanted to be around. He
wanted to be a father, but Ritz couldn't see herself

with him. He was a drug dealer, after all. And young, too young. She had decided she would raise this baby by herself. The way Chip Fields raised Kim and Alexis. Hell, they might be clones for all we knew because those girls looked as if Chip had spit them out, and there was no daddy around and both of them turned out all right, Ritz thought. *My little Madalyn will be just fine.*

Madalyn, in honor of a woman whom Ritz never got a chance to tell just how much she meant to her. Aunt Maddie, perhaps the most understanding, loving example, and the kind of woman that Ritz knew she was incapable of being but might get close to in an attempt to be a mommy. She owed that much to Little Madalyn.

"You're going to get the very best of everything, little girl—including me," Ritz whispered to her baby. "I will never leave you!"

Ritz snuggled her baby gently in her arms. She pulled back the blanket to get a better look at her Little Madalyn. It was the first time Ritz had really got to see her daughter. She stared into a face less than an hour into this world. She had a striking form. Ritz was looking into a mirror when she looked into the face of her baby girl, who had the same pretty, smooth complexion, a few shades lighter. The little girl even looked to have the beginnings of the same deep dimples that Ritz had.

Ritz saw herself for perhaps the first time in her

life. In a pure form. She saw herself in a way she'd never expected. This baby had an innocence that Ritz could hardly identify with, but it seemed to crack open a window inside Ritz. It began to melt that solid-ice-cold heart Ritz had developed over the years. Ritz knew for the first time that she had never known love until this day.

She was madly, wildly in love with her baby.

1

Six months later . . .

The brass urn was positioned on a table in the bay window in the seating area of Ritz's bedroom suite. It sat as a rare artifact, a showcase piece. It had replaced the bassinet that had held court there for so many months until her uncle Cecil begged her to get rid of it.

"Baby, you have to move on," he told her. "Please, Ritzy. Give it to charity. You can't keep torturing yourself like this."

Yes, I can, Ritz said to herself.

So she replaced one symbol of the only thing she ever truly loved with yet another. Ritz allowed Uncle

Cecil to pack up the baby's bed—along with the baby clothes, the Tiffany's silver baby rattle, and the hundreds of other gifts Ritz had received from colleagues, acquaintances, and even fans. He packed it all up and sent it off to Goodwill. But Ritz would never let go of her little girl.

She walked over to the window, picked up the brass urn, and held it. She put it to her ear and shook it gently. It sounded like a baby's rattle. Hard particles were among the ash. She wondered what those things were. Little bone fragments? Tiny teeth? One day, perhaps, her curiosity would get the better of her, and she would open the urn and see what was inside. She would touch what was in there, hoping to feel something again.

She thought about her baby, who shared her face, right down to the dimples, and what she might have wanted to be. Would she have been smart, a doctor or scientist perhaps? Would she have been an actress or a model? During those months after the birth of her child, Ritz had made so many promises. She was going to be there—her career would take a backseat.

She was going to raise her child. There would be no nanny. She was going to teach her how to count, how to read. Ritz imagined all of the mother-daughter conversations she would have with her daughter about life. She would tell her everything she needed to know, and it wouldn't be in the old-fashioned, keeping-secrets way she was raised. There would be no secrets. But none of that was to be.

The last six months had been tough—watching her baby girl fight daily for her life while hooked up to machines, being probed by doctors and specialists. None of them had given her more than a few weeks. It was a rare disease that no adult had survived, let alone a baby. Yet four months later, Little Madalyn Harper was still holding on—a fighter, just like her mother. But she lost her battle.

And Ritz almost checked out with her baby. It was that last card atop a house of cards that threatened to crumble Ritz's entire world.

"What doesn't kill you will only make you stronger," Aunt Maddie had told Ritz on so many occasions that Ritz thought her aunt had created the phrase.

Still, Ritz couldn't get out of bed for two weeks. She was practically catatonic. And every day she remained in bed, another piece of her heart calloused over until the whole thing was just one hard shell.

Nothing could penetrate Ritz Harper's heart again. Nothing was left to hurt—making her more dangerous than ever. She had nothing real to live for, but got up out of that bed under a new kind of energy. It wasn't quite revenge. Because whom would she be getting back at? God? Perhaps. But it was close. She got out of that bed with a new drive, a new determination that could not be stopped. Her career—the one she was willing to walk away from when Little Madalyn was born—would now become her baby.

Ritz Harper would feed and clothe it, put everything she had into it. She would be back on top. And she had a lot of work to do.

So on this night, Ritz would reveal her bold career ambitions to Chas; and if Chas wasn't on the same page, he could keep it moving.

2

Chas James picks up his cell in midstroke to see who was calling. He wasn't going to stop what he was doing; he saw it was Ritz and stopped in his tracks.

"What's the matter, daddy?" said the small, but well-muscled, brown-skinned man who had spent the last fifteen minutes with his face in a pillow while Chas drilled him from behind. "Why'd you stop? It was feeling *so* good!"

Chas, not one for explanations, pulled out. He was rock hard, and instincts and even his body wanted him to finish what he'd started, but there was plenty of time for that. Ritz was calling and he had to call her back. He headed to the bathroom.

"Get dressed," he said dismissively. "I've got something to do. I'll call you."

The small, brown man had just met Chas the night before, but something in his tone let him know he should just dress and wait for a call—one that might not ever come.

Chas took a quick shower and dialed Ritz. He hadn't spoken to her in six months. Ritz had disappeared. She wanted to be left alone, and Chas respected her space. At the same time, he resented being left high and dry. Ritz was his primary source of income. She was his cash cow. Her meteoric rise had helped fund his lifestyle.

Through his salary as Ritz's producer and the lumps of cash he pocketed for her appearances and the other freebies and perks from being in the Ritz circle, Chas was able to build his own mini-empire. He had an apartment in trendy Battery Park Village in a building with a view of the Brooklyn Bridge and the East River. As a kid he used to daydream about this kind of view while looking out his Bronx tenement building into an alleyway.

Chas shared space with captains of industry, dot-com magnates, and a few people who had inherited money from wealthy parents. They called them the invisible rich because unlike the stars and the celebrities, they could walk the streets, and they rarely worried about paparazzi or autograph seekers. And many of them could buy and sell the average celebrity.

Chas loved it. He, too, was one of the invisibles. He put his creation out front to take the limelight, the flashbulbs, and, on one occasion, the bullets. While he collected his paper and did his thing.

His address was downtown, close enough to the Meatpacking District, the Village, and even Chelsea, where he would cruise nightly to feed his voracious appetite for sex. His sex drive was only surpassed by his drive to be wealthy and successful.

But both seemed to be drying up. In the six months of no-Ritz, Chas had been struggling. He hustled, going back into his bag of tricks and promoting parties. But it wasn't nearly the kind of money he was used to, and it wasn't the kind of money that would keep him living the way he had for the last few years.

Ritz was calling. This was good. Very good.

3

She wants to come back? The thought was bittersweet. Sometimes he wished she hadn't come back that first time. Maybe things would have been better for Chas— at least he was willing to bet on it.

As fucked-up as it was to even think, the reality was that Ritz's death would have given Chas a clean slate. The last few years of Ritz's rise had been messy, to say the least. Careers and lives had been ruined. Enemies were around every corner. There were few people whom Ritz hadn't outed, ridiculed, jacked up, or messed over. Her death would have been poetic. For

Chas, it would have been cleansing and a tremendous opportunity.

Shot down in a hail of bullets on a public New York City street, wearing one of her best furs, at the top of her game—the kind of story you would only find in a book or on the big screen. *It would have been perfect,* thought Chas.

He already had the public relations plan ready to go: Did gossip kill the Queen of Radio? Was freedom of speech being assassinated? Ritz would become an urban legend. Tapes from her last *Ritz Harper Excursion* show would become cult classics. Chas would become an overnight sensation. He'd give interviews all over the world about their last show. He would be like Puffy on the heels of Biggie's murder.

Chas would host the most fabulous hot-pink-and-leopard-themed public memorial. He'd wear a ribbon and become a public advocate for free speech on the airwaves. And when he grew tired of the marches and the memorials, he'd pen a tell-all book about how Ritz was playing Russian roulette with her life all along and why he'd predicted her untimely death was only a matter of time . . .

But the bitch lived! And now she was calling on Chas to help her mount yet another comeback.

Not too long ago Chas James was the most envied man in the industry. He'd groomed Ritz Harper. He was her Pygmalion, minus the eventual love story. But he'd formed her out of nothing—at least that's the story he told himself. But just as Pygmalion's Galatea was formed out of ivory, Ritz began as something pretty special, just in need of a little direction. Chas certainly provided the direction and the vision, but Ritz had to possess something in order to execute.

Ritz's lack of shame and her strange sense of self-righteousness allowed her to say the things she did on the airwaves. And her audience appreciated not just the shock value, but the honesty.

When she cooed about a music mogul's sex romp with one of his *male* rappers, Ritz did so primarily because she was sick of seeing him parade around as if he were a family man, and a ladies' man.

". . . and that goes out to Mr. Ladies' Man himself! Yeah right! If you want to see the truth, y'all check out my Web site. I have pictures! *Oooooh, how you doin'?!*"

Most days Ruffin would sit in his office cringing while listening to the *Excursion*. It was the car accident he couldn't keep from rubbernecking to see. This was not how he wanted to spend the twilight years of his career, presiding over garbage such as this. He would call Chas in weekly to discuss the direction of the show, and when Ritz would go too far, he would threaten suspension. But Ruff knew his hands were tied. Radio was a business, and one on the downturn at that, with the emergence of satellite, Internet, and iPods.

"Chas, you better rein her in!" he would say. "If I

get one more threat of a lawsuit, I'm pulling the plug!"

But even Chas knew that Ruff didn't have the balls to pull the plug. He may have hated the show, he may even have hated Ritz at times, but he and his station loved the revenue she generated.

But in the last few months, Ritz wasn't bringing home the bacon. She was home in mourning. And as Janet said, "What have you done for me lately . . ." Ritz's star had faded and her queendom was under attack. It was easy for Ruff to forget what she had been because, well, Ritz was turning out to be a has-been. She couldn't get herself out of bed, and even her fans were showing themselves to be fair-weather.

So when Ruff got the call from Chas that Ritz was coming back, he wasn't welcoming her with open arms. He was enjoying the break from Ritz.

The drive-by shooting and those months off the air actually kept the station on top with the constant media attention, updates, and reports. Everybody loves a victim and Ritz was the victim du jour. She came back from the shooting to anticipation and loads of backed-up venom. Ritz was more ferocious than ever with her new lease on life and determination to make whoever shot her pay with even more success and over-the-top commentary.

When it was announced she was pregnant, Ritz went from gossiper to subject as speculation swirled around who was her baby's daddy. Ritz actually loved being in the middle of that fire and would pour gasoline on it every chance she got. And the ratings for the *Excursion* went through the roof.

But when she lost little Madalyn, she changed. Everything changed. After a couple of months of sympathy waned; people were itchy for another Ritz Harper comeback. But it never came. There wasn't even a Ritz Harper sighting anywhere. People started to forget. They had overdosed on Ritz Harper and gone into recovery and seemed to have kicked their Ritz Harper habit.

A parade of up-and-coming radio personalities were waiting to take Ritz's throne.

Now the queen wanted to come back. And Chas had to bring Ritz back to prove his worth as a producer. Ritz was *his* star, and he had to make her shine again—for his own sake.

The two had been inseparable at one time. Once, Chas and Ritz could finish each other's sentences. They were so close they could practically read each other's mind. Their relationship was organic. But she got huge and changed; he got jealous and changed. And drama happened. Neither of them saw the fork in the road coming, and it blindsided them.

But now Chas had to somehow get them back in the same car, heading in the same direction. He had to.

4

Masa, an exquisite windowless restaurant nestled inside the Time Warner Center, was akin to a Japanese temple. Minimalist design, cool colors, and cloak-wearing servers set the divine backdrop for New York's elite to experience the sushi of the gods.

There were no cell phones here. No menus. The chef, Masa Takayama, prepared what he deemed would be your feast for the night. The two-hour meal was guaranteed to be unforgettable—and at $1,000 per person, Masa Takayama never disappointed.

Most who visited the bustling mall never made it

inside the twenty-six-seat restaurant; and only New York royalty could secure a last-minute table for two. Yet Chas pulled a few strings—the perks of sucking and fucking all the right men—to treat the tragic Queen of Radio to five-star sushi and priceless tranquillity. Chas knew that illusion and, more often than not, the delusion of grandeur was a powerful drug. Ritz could never know how far he had fallen. But more important, she could never know how far *she* had fallen.

By the looks of her, she hadn't a clue. Ritz breezed into Zen with the grace of a gazelle and the air of royalty. She sported a simple black Chanel suit with eighteen-karat yellow gold and diamond-framed shades. The shades were sleek and small, barely covering her large doe eyes.

"Chanel, baby, from head to toe," Chas cooed. "I love it!"

Ritz adored how much of a girlfriend Chas could be. She missed that part of their relationship. But she knew their relationship was on the brink of a change. Tonight was not about getting reacquainted, it was about making moves and taking things in a whole other direction.

"Yes and no," Ritz said. "The glasses are number 23 style, Luxuriator."

"Really?" Chas feigned adoration for a brand he knew nothing about. How had the student surpassed the master? Ritz used to wear off-the-rack duds, until he showed her how to dress like a star.

So what the fuck are Luxuriators? And who introduced her to that brand?

The sunglasses cost more than the suit, and they were a test to see if Chas was on his game. Ritz needed to know if Chas knew the brand she was rocking, or if he was out of his league. And if he was out of his league, would he be man enough to admit it? And if he couldn't, could she still trust him? If he could pretend with her over something as silly as a brand, then would he lie about something big that could cost her? She needed to trust him.

A whisper interrupts the moment of truth.

"Lemon-water finger bowls," said the pale, immaculately groomed server. "Your starter meal is being prepared."

"Starter meal? Hmmm. How befitting," said Ritz. "A starter meal for my starter life."

Chas was also starting over—on Ritz's tattered coattails.

"So are you ready to return? WHOT is ready to have you back," Chas lied.

"Well, I'm not ready to go back to WHOT. Back is backwards," Ritz said coolly. "I want to go to the next level. I want television."

The waif server methodically removed the lemon-water finger bowls and set the table with bamboo utensils. Just as suddenly, he became one with the air and vanished.

"Television?! Ritz, are you out of your mind?" Chas raised his voice a little louder than he intended.

"What the fuck, Chas?" said Ritz, getting visibly angry. "You think I'm not good enough or something?"

"Um, I-I just prepared for your return to our show," he said, trying to recover. "Your listeners miss you. It's been a frenzy over there."

Ritz caressed the lacquered bamboo utensil between her fingers.

"Chas, I was thinking, what if I didn't make it? What if everything ended right there on that New York City street. Perhaps I was spared to do something else. Something bigger. I thought raising Madalyn would be it."

"Go on," Chas said, trying to seem intrigued.

"Mothers are not supposed to outlive their children," she said, feeling herself being pulled back into that dark, sad place. "I held my daughter. I looked into her face. I saw me in that face. And I made a pact to sacrifice everything I own and ever wanted for her. For the first time I was letting someone in, Chas.

"And what does God do? He allows Madalyn to live long enough to show me that I *could* let someone in. And that changed me. Then I lose her. So now what, Chas? Now what? I can't come back to the same old thing because I'm not the same old Ritz. I have to take the stakes higher. I have to have more. I have to be more."

Chas was shaking his head. Did she really think she was going to walk away from WHOT and land a gig on television? She was hardly wanted back at the radio station. Ritz was toxic. Now Chas was sure she was also delusional. Losing her mind.

"I'm telling you this as your producer and your friend," Chas said gingerly. "You've had a lot of trauma. It's wearing on your face, and until you can get yourself tight again, yours is a face for radio. On TV, you can't hide depression or even a long night on the town behind thirty-five-hundred-dollar Luxuriator shades."

"I want a television talk show," said Ritz, unfazed. "I want a studio audience so that I can see who I'm talking to, and they can see me."

"What will they be looking at? The Queen of Radio in a free fall?"

Ritz sucked her teeth. So here it was, Chas's pussy envy manifesting itself, Ritz thought.

"Here's the deal, Ritz: You can bounce back or bow out," he warned. "But you don't start over. Not at this level of the game. I can't be at your side for this bullshit fantasy of yours."

"My thoughts exactly!" Ritz bit back.

Chas, realizing that Ritz was actually willing to move on without him, backed up.

"Ritz, let's talk about this," he said more calmly. "Why television? Why now? Do you realize how difficult things are going to be once you leave one career to jump-start another?"

Ritz removed her shades and rubbed her eyes, unconsciously smearing her eye makeup. Her enormous brown eyes were ablaze against the smudged kohl-black eyeliner and red-fox-fur extension eyelashes.

"I know I can do this, Chas. And what bothers me is that you can't see it."

"I know how hard we've worked to bring you to this point, and I know that you really can't—"

"Can't what?!" she said now, almost shouting. "Get to the next level? That's the fucking problem! You don't believe in me?!"

The server appeared out of nowhere and whispered, "Please keep your voices to a minimum. You are interrupting the ambience."

Chas nodded in agreement. Ritz stared him down.

"Bring the food already," she growled. "I'm starving!"

The server bowed and vanished.

"Ritz, this is the kind of spot that I'd like to return to, so please, let's not do this here."

"Chas, I appreciate what you've done for me, I won't forget that. But there's so much more to do. I think that you're not ready for television, that you don't have the connects or the heart, so you don't want me to do it."

"I have connects," Chas managed. "I have plenty—"

"Then put me in a room with them. Let me show what I have to offer. Either roll with me or get the fuck out of the way, Chas!"

Chas slammed his hand on the table, sending a bamboo utensil to the floor. "Get the fuck out of the way? I am the way! I showed you the way!" he yelled. "You didn't have shit going on before I came along. Don't fucking forget that."

"Did I slide out of your pussy, Chas? What makes you think that I would not have accomplished this without you? It's not like you found me in the gutter, as some talentless bitch. Get over this God complex! So, yeah, either come with me and let's do this together, or get the fuck out of the way!"

The server returned; this time he asked Chas and Ritz to leave.

Chas rose and placed a few C-notes in the server's hand. "Please send my regrets to the chef," he whispered in the server's ear. "We meant no disrespect."

Ritz remained seated and in full tantrum mode. "I want to eat something. I've been sitting here and my stomach is stuck to my fucking back!"

"Okay, okay, calm down," Chas said. "Let's go out into the mall and grab a bite."

"And I want to meet with the studios, Chas. And I'm not going back to WHOT until I do."

"Okay, Ritz," he sighed. "I'll make a few calls."

Ritz wasn't ready for television and neither was he—but Chas had to take Ritz to Hollywood or he was a failure. Funny how Ritz Harper's success was her own but her failure was theirs to share.

Chas knew there was only one man to call—Rutger Blake.

5

Rutger punched in the seven-digit code that unlocked the safe behind the false wall in the bookcase of his library. He took out the mahogany case and added the final coin to complete the Chinese lunar-series gold collection. He had a complete set of the Australian Philharmonic. He had a set of the buffalo series that had become so scarce in 2008 that the government stopped minting them, but the Chinese lunar series was the prize of his gold collection, primarily because the Chinese had lost so much faith in the dollar that they were buying up gold as if it were water, making his collection worth four times what he'd purchased it at.

He put the heavy box holding his coins back into his deep safe, alongside his palladium, platinum, and rare-diamond collections—worth just a little more than $10 million. He loved the liquidity and that the value would be the same no matter what country or land he traveled; from the Middle East to the middle of Germany, an ounce of gold traded for the same, as did the diamond, platinum, and palladium.

Rutger loved the power money bought. He understood that at an early age, and it was why he'd set his sights on the most powerful medium of them all—the media and entertainment. Whoever controlled images and the delivery of those images to the masses could literally control the world.

Rutger Blake earned his MBA in media and entertainment, with a concentration in advertising, from the Media School at Bournemouth University in the U.K. Soon thereafter, Rutger moved to New York to work for Silver Screen Motion Pictures, a theater-management company run by his uncle. Recognizing that audiences wanted to see the previews—which were mere commercials for upcoming releases—Rutger thought, why not show this captive audience exciting commercials for products?

Rutger monetized Silver Screen Motion Pictures by partnering with major corporations and introducing advertisements before the previews. He added yet another stream of revenue by partnering with the music industry to play selected artists before the pre-preview advertisements.

Rutger was named president and CEO of Silver Screen Motion Pictures, and he soon infiltrated network television by acquiring the catalogs of classic television shows and investing in the development and syndication of new reality-television shows. As Rutger was building his empire, the big four networks—ABC, CBS, NBC, and FOX—were losing an uphill battle with cable television. Cable television offered diversified content to viewers; enjoyed more artistic freedom (without interference from the FCC, the Federal Communications Commission); won more awards; and thus commanded more cross-branding advertising revenue.

Realizing the power in numbers, the big four networks joined forces to create the Big Four to compete with cable by challenging the strict FCC rules, creating more quality programming, and offering late-night adult television content at competitive rates.

The network alliance was built on trust, and a visionary leader was needed to produce new entertainment while preserving each network's own brand identity.

The blue-eyed Brit was the man for the job.

With a growing portfolio of hot acquisitions under his belt, Rutger was recruited to serve as chairman of the board of the Big Four. No script was approved, no actor was hired, and no project was given the green light without Rutger's stamp of approval. Since Rutger had taken the helm, the networks had enjoyed a surge in viewing audiences and a spike in profits.

The unassuming, thirtysomething Brit with the slight smile and the five-o'clock shadow had become the most powerful man in network television. And the most ruthless man in Hollywood.

In media, Rutger was a mad genius. In his personal life, Rutger was a madman. Rutger was not a lover. Or a friend. Rutger was a collector. He didn't view people as equals; he considered them to be mere toys. Someone, rather, some thing would excite Rutger, and he would capture it with his wealth and perfect promises.

Once he'd satisfied his curiosity, he'd toss his toy aside and move on to another. But Chas James was one toy that whenever Rutger tossed it to the side, he always came back to play with him again and again. It was Chas who had had enough the last time Rutger had used him for his own amusement and then didn't call again for a year. Chas had promised himself he would never again get caught in Rutger's web.

But now he needed a favor. . . .

6

If Jamie didn't have bad luck, she'd have no luck at all. First Ritz Harper, her spoiled-rotten, self-important bitch of an ex-boss, gets shot and dies. Then she has the audacity to be revived and become even more of a spoiled-rotten, self-important bitch of a boss. WHOT was doing well with FOX newswoman Michelle Davis manning the *Ritz Harper Excursion* show, and Jamie could actually see light at the end of the tunnel.

Being an associate producer for Michelle meant ascension, it meant getting one step closer to her goal. But, wham! Ritz was back from the brink of death and taping the number one drive-time show (oh, yeah, they were syndicated in thirty states) from her home. And Jamie was forced to move in with Ritz! There was no more leaving the degradation at the job; now she had to fuse her home life with her work life if she wanted to stay on the *Excursion* team. And Jamie really did; that was the reality about glamour jobs . . . the stars in your eyes often masked the diminishing returns.

When things couldn't get worse, Derek, her irresistible, sexy, mature roughneck, dumped her for no reason at all. So there she was, slaving for the Queen, living in her palace, and having no indication that things would ever get better.

Jamie had never met a beast like Ritz Harper before—someone who had everything, and always wanted more. Someone so insatiable. Someone who was never satisfied.

Ritz's outrageous demands grew worse after she got pregnant. She stayed on the air up until the day she had her baby girl. Soon thereafter, Ritz announced to the crew that she was in love with her baby and would be no longer holding down the *Excursion*! The sun was shining again for Jamie.

FOX News reporter Michelle Davis began filling the spot with her own show and was later told by Fox to choose: News or WHOT. Michelle didn't blink twice when she told WHOT of her decision to stay behind the mic.

The crew, Ritz's producer, Chas, Aaron the engineer, and Jamie loved Michelle. Ruffin, the station manager, was keen on the intelligent, uplifting conversations and topics that Michelle brought to the show. She was a strong advocate for education, and a breath of fresh air. Ruffin had been in the business long enough to know that WHOT really needed to take a new approach with the afternoon drive time, too. Things were going so well, then, wham! Ritz's baby died.

And now the bitch was back.

Jamie jump-started her plans to get out of Ritz's way. With Ritz on her way back, Jamie's ascension would be halted, and she knew it. She had to force her own good luck, and she did it by investing her money in stocks and bonds and securing employment as a market analyst at Smith Barney, an investment firm.

Things were going as planned. On Monday, September 15, Jamie was called for her second interview; on Thursday, September 18, Jamie was hired and given her employment packet. That Friday, Jamie reported to work. As Aaron counted down to the start of the show, Jamie boldly blurted to Ritz, "This is my official two-week notice!" *Take that Ritz Harper!*

"What?!" Ritz was not used to being blindsided. She had futuristic vision and always saw one or two steps ahead. But her vision had been cloudy of late. She hadn't seen the bullets. She didn't expect to get pregnant. She certainly didn't see the death of her aunt, who'd raised her, or that of her very own baby girl, who was named after her. She didn't see any of this coming. And Jamie's sucker punch felt like the straw that would break Ritz's back.

"The little fucking ingrate," Ritz seethed to herself.

But the diva couldn't let anyone see her sweat.

"I'm so happy for you." Ritz was so phony that even she couldn't believe it. "We all wish you well, Jamie."

Jamie smiled. But inside she knew Ritz's Ms. Nice Guy act was just that. But Ritz couldn't do anything to her now, Jamie thought. So for the following week she had a little pep in her step as she removed the remnants of being Ritz Harper's lackey. She was darn near whistling a happy tune as she neared her final days under Ritz's thumb.

On Friday, September 26, Ritz had a little going-away prize for Jamie. They were nearing the end of the final hour of the show, and Ritz sidled up to the mic, getting close and intimate as she did when she was about to drop a bomb on her audience.

"I want to thank someone very special to our team here at the *Excursion*," Ritz began. "Jamie has been with us for the last few years, and she has seen us through so much. But she will be leaving us. We're going to miss her, everybody!"

Ritz told Aaron off-mic to cue up Diana Ross's slow "Missing You."

"So where are you going, Jamie?" Ritz asked, motioning her to pull up to the guest mic. Jamie couldn't believe it. Ritz Harper, the cow that never shared her spotlight or her mic, was thanking her for a job well done and allowing her to give a few shout-outs on her last day? WOW! *Maybe the Ice Queen did have a heart.*

"I'm heading over to Smith Barney," Jamie said. "I've been hired as a market analyst. I'm very excited and I thank you for the opportunity, Ritz."

Ritz shot Jamie a look that she had seen before. Ritz had a smile on her face, but behind the smile in her eyes were shards of glass. Jamie had seen the contrast quite often, right before Ritz went in for the kill, like a vampire right before sinking its teeth into an unsuspecting victim.

Jamie's blood grew cold. She knew what was coming next: humiliation. Dangerous, embarrassing, no-holds-barred gossip. Aaron keyed up Prince's "Scandalous," laying the sound track to Ritz's sneak attack.

"And I want to thank you, Jamie," Ritz said, cutting her off before she was able to get out another word. "I want to thank you for serving up the most delicious meal I ever had in your man, Derek. I really understood why you were so in love with him. That boy really knows how to put it down. That's probably how I got pregnant. That was his beautiful little girl—our baby girl. Well. That really feels good to get that off my chest. You can't imagine how hard it's been coming in here every day and having you living with me knowing I was sleeping with your man. I felt so guilty. Now we can part ways with the air all cleared. I don't know about you, but I feel like I just dropped twenty pounds."

Aaron had his finger on the button to censor the string of cuss words that were sure to follow, but there were none. Jamie's silence said volumes.

Ritz was disappointed, expecting more of a reaction, and decided to bait her.

"Oh, come on, you know he only dated you to get to the Queen, right?" she cooed.

Jamie broke down. Her bottom lip began to quiver as she clenched her jaw, trying to hold back the floodgate, but she couldn't. The dam broke and the tears came in a rush. It was as if Jamie's very soul were in pain and she sobbed, snot and all.

Aaron was supposed to cue up Beyoncé's "Irreplaceable," but he couldn't do it. He'd had a crush on Jamie once upon a time, and seeing her in so much agony bothered him. He had seen Ritz do many cruel things, many of which he'd actually egged on and encouraged, but she had crossed the line with him today. This was too much. She had gone too far, even for Ritz Harper.

"Well, it's Friday, September twenty-sixth, and that's it for the *Ritz Harper Excursion*," she said. "I love you for listening! Have a funky weekend, everybody. And, Jamie, how you doin'?"

Ruffin, the studio manager, cringed. He pushed his Aeron chair away from his desk in disgust. He despised Ritz's antics, especially when she railroaded common, everyday people. Jamie worked for her, lived with her, catered to her, and Ritz still dogged her out like that? That was horrible enough, indeed, but that wasn't the primary reason that the stunt bothered him. Ruff knew that these Ritz antics would earn higher ratings. Ritz Harper knew exactly what she was doing.

The clip of Jamie sobbing would become an instant "Best Of" contender, and the downloads from the Web audience would make it last forever. This was not a good scenario if he wanted to dethrone the Queen. If Ritz had good numbers the Three Suits, that is, the conglomerate that owned the radio station, and Abigail Gogel, the station head in name only, wouldn't touch her.

And Ritz would only get worse—if that was possible.

Jamie stormed out of the studio and raced to Derek's house, for what she wasn't sure. She wanted to confront him. She wanted to look into his eyes and see for herself if the stuff Ritz had said was true. Jamie knew deep inside that it was all true, but she wanted Derek to tell her. And she wanted to know why.

7

Ritz Harper had really fucked him good this time. Derek, the redhead, redbone dope dealer to the stars, had studied enough gangsta films to know that if he didn't go incognito, a bullet would be his end.

Derek's older brother, Jayrod, was doing time because of the mouth of Ritz Harper.

After their mother overdosed, Jayrod raised and nurtured Derek like his own son. And the living was good, while they were supplying and serving pharmaceuticals to the stars. But then Ritz Harper entered their life. Ritz made frequent commentaries on the

Excursion about how the dope game fused with the rap game, and the feds were listening. Jayrod got caught and ended up serving fifteen years to life for racketeering.

Jayrod wanted Ritz's head for it.

Staying true to the family creed, he ordered Derek to do the deed. But Ritz Harper had told Jayrod and the whole world that Derek didn't do the deed. Jayrod had assumed that the hit put on Ritz, those bullets that pierced the diva, had come at his brother's command. They had to have. Jayrod wanted Ritz dead, and his brother always followed through. That she survived was just luck on her part. But Jayrod had had no reason to believe that this baby brother didn't do it, until this day.

Jayrod was even more furious.

"That bitch put me in here and that motherfucker gave her a shorty?" he said to his cellie. "My own flesh and blood crossed me for some pussy? I hope he savored it. His days of fucking are numbered."

During their formative years in the dope game, Derek and Jayrod watched the *Godfather* trilogy at least twice a year to learn the tenets of successful gangsterism.

The brothers learned life's lessons through the eyes of Michael Corleone.

Their eyes were watching the same movies, but their brains were registering very different lessons. For

Jayrod, the reckless spirit, the *Godfather* taught him to live in *the now* because nothing was guaranteed and every moment was to be lived to the fullest—never mind the consequence.

For Derek, the cautious spirit, the *Godfather* taught him to plan for *the next*. One had to accept the unpredictable nature of the now and, in doing so, must always prepare for the next, and Derek lusted for long-term security.

What the two brothers did agree on, however, were the lessons of family loyalty: Early on in the film, Michael warned his older brother, Fredo, "Never take sides against the family." When Fredo double-crossed Michael, Michael killed him.

Jayrod and Derek agreed that Michael was right to do so.

"If you can't trust your own flesh and blood," Jayrod would say each time they watched Fredo get whacked, "that motherfucker needs to die."

By sleeping with Ritz Harper, Derek had become Fredo, and he knew that Jayrod wouldn't think twice about whacking him.

Buy. Sell. Buy. Stash.

Repeat.

The more Derek looked at his life, the more he realized that he lived in the now. And the now was vicious and all-consuming.

Buy the shit from shady individuals.

Sell the shit to shady celebrities.

Buy items that made him feel worthy. Stash money for a rainy day; and in the dope game it always rained when you least expected it.

The now made no promises of security.

Derek could show up to buy the shit and get robbed. He could show up to sell the shit and get stiffed, or even arrested. And he could buy something nice for himself, only to need that extra money for an emergency.

And so it went.

Ritz Harper, his secret, elusive lover, was a welcomed interruption to the monotony that his life had become. The mischievous couple would fuck against the wall of Ritz's home. They rarely made it to the bedroom. Her long legs would wrap around his torso, her arms would hug him so close, her neck would repeatedly fall onto the pathway of Derek's relentless, warm kisses.

Ritz felt so good to him, so right, so natural, and Derek wanted more of her.

Ritz was an independent woman who could be a bitch at work, a siren on the radio, and a submissive freak who wasn't afraid to step out of her panties and let him bounce her around during their raunchy rodeo.

Derek knew that Ritz was pregnant before she knew it. It was a weird connection, as if a zap of electricity had traveled between them. Derek felt it, and at that very moment Ritz stared deep into his eyes to confirm that she felt it, too.

Derek wanted to pull out, he knew he was *supposed* to, but how could he when everything about Ritz Harper was pulling him in?

They were straight sexin', no doubt about that, but their passion had reached a destination where the fucking stopped and the lovemaking began.

Creating a daughter, seeing his daughter, then having her ripped away from him changed everything. He yearned for the next now more than ever, and he wanted Ritz to be at his side.

Who was this woman that beguiled him so? What was it about this woman that conquered his mind and heart?

One thing Derek knew for sure was that he was not caught up in the rapture of Ritz's celebrity—not by a long shot.

Derek was a dealer to the stars. He served women that the average man would kill to meet. Derek routinely served celebrity hotties in their VIP parties, in their homes, and in their limos. He saw them in various degrees of drug-induced euphoria and in various stages of undress. But the coke-, heroin-, and meth-using little vixens never enticed him.

Ritz Harper, however, had his full attention.

But now she had sealed his fate.

Derek paced the floor of his quaint apartment

roaming from room to room looking for something to pack. He didn't know where he was going, but he knew he couldn't stay put.

Derek's body was one big oxymoron: His mouth was dry, his hands were sweaty. He was hot, then cold; his stomach was churning although he hadn't eaten all day. He was breathless at times and had to rest, only to feel his heartbeat thumping at double the speed.

Derek tore apart his closets and pulled out his favorite outfits, too many to pack at one time, but he took what he could—shoes, watches, sweaters, jewelry. He tossed the expensive items about, making piles in order of importance: things he had to have, things he'd like to have, and things he could do without.

The luggage set had been tucked away in the walk-in closet since he and Jayrod took that trip to Vegas. It had been five years now. *Damn, time travels fast.*

Derek grabbed a suitcase and a matching duffel bag. He laid them in the center of the bedroom. That's when it hit him—the two luggage pieces represented two different options. Derek could take the road trip to the penitentiary and plead his case to Jayrod: "I know I was supposed to kill her, but I love her . . ."

Or Derek could hit the open road and try to start a new life somewhere else, somewhere his brother couldn't exact revenge. Derek's brother knew people that owed him favors, too many of them to count. There were few places Derek could go where Jayrod didn't know somebody willing to do Jayrod the ultimate favor.

The thought of fleeing his own flesh and blood triggered a wave of uncomfortable memories of Jayrod. Derek wondered which of Jayrod's homeboys would be hired to kill him.

He reached on the top shelf to retrieve his .45 automatic pistol. He checked the ammo, engaged the safety lock, and tucked the gun into his back pocket. The doorbell rang, shattering Derek's frenzied silence.

Derek was frozen.

The doorbell rang again.

Derek was so still, he held his breath.

Perhaps it was just the mailman, or more likely, the hit man. Maybe they didn't know he was home.

The bell rang a third time, this time accompanied by loud knocks on the door.

Derek was terror-struck. Derek pulled out his gun from his back pocket. He disengaged the safety lock and crept to his own front door.

"I know you're home, Derek!" Jamie yelled as she simultaneously banged on the door and rang the bell. "Let me in! I ain't got nowhere to go, I will stay out here as long as I need to!"

Derek produced a long, heavy sigh, engaged the safety lock, and returned the gun to his back pocket. "Stop knocking. Hold on!"

"Yeah, I'll hold on!" Jamie yelled. "Open the fucking door!"

Derek was running out of time. The last thing he needed was to talk to Jamie. She was loud and mad and one false move and his neighbors would call the police. Derek had to get out of town, he didn't have time for this.

He opened the door.

"This ain't a good time, J, come back tomorrow," he said curtly.

Jamie opened her lungs and screamed from her belly, "Oh hell *no*! Tell that little ho you with to get out. We gotta talk. Don't play with me."

Derek grabbed Jamie by the collar and yanked her inside.

"Don't make a scene, J, don't even do it. You got five minutes."

Derek shut the door and locked it. The young woman adjusted her collar and faced him, arms crossed, eyes bloodshot.

"I heard the show, trust me," Derek offered. "I didn't think you'd come over here."

"And why the fuck not? You owe me an explanation."

"I owe you an explanation?" Derek was ready to argue, but he thought better of it. Why take the time to win an argument with Jamie—only to get snuffed out by a hired hit man later? He had to get out of there.

"You're right, J, I fucked up. I'm sorry," Derek said, using his body to block the pathway to the front room. "Ritz didn't mean shit to me. I'm really sorry."

Jamie sensed his urgency to put her out, so she planned to linger. She planned to be there if Ritz stopped by to fuck him after work.

"What's up, Derek?" Jamie brushed past him, bumping him as hard as she could.

"You know what's up, J. Look, I'm not in the mood, not tonight."

"Oh, really?" she said, kicking off her shoes and planting her behind firmly on his couch. "Because I'm in the mood, Derek. Tell me a story."

"About what?" Derek picked up Jamie's shoes and placed them on her lap. "You can't stay. I'm in the middle of something."

She threw the shoes across the room. "Tell me about how you dumped me and had a baby with my boss. That's the story I wanna hear." Jamie stretched out and unbuttoned her jeans. "And I'm not going nowhere until you tell me something."

Derek knew Jamie well enough to know that she wasn't leaving. He wanted her to leave as much as she wanted to stay, and there were no two ways about it. He could break her heart, but it wouldn't send her scurrying out the door; she'd want to hang around and fight. Perhaps break some shit. Perhaps get him thrown in the county jail so that one of his brother's homeys could shank him as he slept.

"Why are you looking at me that way?" she crowed. "Open your mouth and talk. What's wrong? Ritz's pussy got you tongue-tied?"

"I don't know what you want me to say, J. Honestly, I don't know why you came here."

"So you caught your baby mama's little stunt?"

Derek withdrew the gun from his pocket and checked the safety lock. He laid it on top of the television set. Only then did he notice Jamie's wide eyes.

"Oh, it was bothering me, weighing down my pocket, you know how that is."

"Why do you have a gun, Derek? What's going on?"

Derek joined Jamie on the couch. He scanned her, head to waist and then up again. He used to like her . . . so why did he dislike her so much now? Her timing was off, Jamie's timing was always off. She came around at the wrong time, always, and tonight was no different, with the exception that this was her absolute worst timing of all.

"J, if you want to talk about this, we can, just this once. Then I don't want to bring it up anymore. Remember, my daughter died, too. I don't wanna go back to that."

Jamie changed her tone and body language. A loaded gun tended to bring out the calm in drama queens.

"You cooled it with me so that you could creep with her. Why? Is it because she got money? Derek, she's old as hell, I don't understand."

Derek crossed his arms to block Jamie's bullshit. "She's not that old. She's just a few years older than us, and she's sexy."

"You dumped me because she's sexy? Derek, I thought you were better than that, always talking about the business, and having a strategy behind the struggle, and you mix it up with Ritz?"

Actually, Ritz had mixed him up. Derek was going to leave the drug game, the life, *one day*, but Ritz had forced his time and he had to do it now.

"You've got it wrong, J. I didn't leave you for her, it didn't happen that way. It was just a bad timing for you. I've always had a crush on her. I would see her here and there, when I was at some events working, you know."

Jamie sucked her bottom lip. "So, you ever serve her?"

"No. Never. She was there working, doing her radio thang and I was slanging . . . but that was it."

"That bitch is head-to-toe fake, she even got fake body parts. We're nothing alike, Derek. That shit don't make sense. How can you want her and want me?"

"Because I don't want you anymore, not in that way."

Jamie unbuttoned her blouse. "I'm thirsty."

"I don't have anything for you to drink here, J. I told you, don't get comfortable."

"You can give Ritz a daughter but I can't get some water?!" Jamie yelled.

Derek huffed and puffed and finally went into the kitchen. He had an ice-cold bottle of FIJI in the fridge, but she was not getting that. Derek fumbled in the cabinet for a clean glass. He found one and filled it with warm tap water.

When he reentered the front room, Jamie was waiting for him—naked.

"You know you miss this pussy," she purred.

"Put your clothes back on and get out, J. For real!"

She put her hands on her hips. Derek's dick got hard without his permission and it angered him.

"Put your clothes on," he said firmly. "And go home!"

"I don't think you remember us. Fuck me first. And if you can leave me after that, then you don't have to worry about me no more."

Derek threw the warm water in her face. "Get your clothes on and get out!"

"You wet my hair? How could you?!"

Jamie started to cry. She cried so hard that her body convulsed. She plopped back on the couch and retrieved her clothes between long bouts of sniveling. Derek preferred a pissed-off Jamie storming out, not a brokenhearted Jamie prolonging a painful exit. He left the front room and returned with a towel. He blotted her hair, and her face, smearing her makeup.

"It ain't you, for real," he said. "It's a lot of shit goin' on with me, girl. I'm sorry."

"I just can't believe you dumped me for her, Derek," Jamie bawled. "Do you know that now she has taken everything from me? Even you."

Jamie pulled up her jeans to her knees. Then she

stood up to wiggle and slide them over her ass. She put on her shoes. Derek couldn't resist looking at her round, brown ass. She was petite, but power-stacked.

At that moment, Jamie had sexy down to a science—topless, tight jeans, and heels. If Jamie were a different type of girl, she'd make a good living as a video vixen. Jamie was such a cute girl to him; and that was the problem, he wanted a woman. He wanted Ritz.

Derek situated himself on the couch to conceal the telltale erection.

She spied it anyway. "How could you just sit there with a rock-hard dick and not even touch me? Am I ugly to you or something?"

"Never, J!"

Jamie fastened her bra and grabbed her blouse. "Then tell me. Just tell me."

"Tell you what, *exactly*?"

"Tell me why you chose her over me."

"I was just being a dog, just doing what a dog does when he's tempted," he lied. "I wasn't choosing her over you, I was just choosing. I didn't think about what would happen next. I didn't think about hurting you, I really didn't expect you to ever find out. I thought that because she was crossing you, too, that we had an honor among thieves that she'd be too ashamed to ever tell on herself."

"And you ran up in her without a rubber, Derek?"

He just sat there shaking his head. "I fucked up,

real bad. I only hit her one time, and the rubber broke on me. I don't know if that baby was mine or not. She never let me see the baby, and the next thing I know, she said the baby died. What kind of bullshit is that? I think she was lying all along."

Jamie nodded in agreement. "She probably was."

Derek placed his arm around Jamie. "Look, I have some business I need to take care of, and I'll be gone for a minute. When I'm back, we'll talk. We'll, you know, do what needs to be done so that you can at least trust me again."

Jamie gave him that look. "I want some, baby."

Derek smiled. "I want some, too, as you can tell. But I've got to get out of here right quick. You know, business first. And then you will be the first person I call when I come back."

"Where are you going?"

"The more you don't know, the better it is for both of us. Trust me. Look, I don't want Ritz. I'm never hooking up with her again, ever. And I'll handle you as soon as I get back, okay, J?"

"You promise?"

"My word is bond," Derek lied again.

He tilted his head to give Jamie a peck on the cheek, and she quickly turned her face to catch his kiss on her lips. She waited longingly for another. But Derek rose from the couch, hinting for her to meet him at the door. Jamie got the hint.

"Stop all that crying, you spoiled brat!" Derek teased as Jamie *finally* left his apartment.

"Don't forget to call me, Derek."

Derek shut the door and bolted it.

Jamie's bruised ego enhanced the effectiveness of Derek's performance. In her mind, of course, he only slept with Ritz once. Of course, the rubber broke. Of course, the baby could or could not have been his child.

Of course, he'd call when he returned.

Jamie really liked Derek, and she really hated Ritz. Human nature dictated that Jamie should have been wrecked by the double betrayal. But outside forces were working against an imminent heartbreak.

Jamie, much like many young working women, felt obligated to seize the spotlight (before the competition did). Coupled with the lack of face time in their technology-driven relationships, their tunnel vision for success was secure. Jamie's ambition shielded her from devastation. A good cry followed by Derek's good lie was all she needed to move on. The women of Jamie's generation had learned to date like men.

Besides, ruminating over each relationship betrayal could result in career immobility.

And there was no time for that.

Jamie returned to her parents' home. That weekend, she got her stuff and herself together and attempted to put all of the unpleasantness, betrayal, and pain behind her as she got ready for her new life.

She would be at her new gig on Monday and she

would find a new man. *There are plenty of fish in the sea, right?* But Jamie also knew she wasn't interested in any of those fish. She couldn't stop feeling what she was feeling for Derek.

She would pour herself into her new career. She vowed she would focus on building her wealth. Jamie would have so much money that she would one day buy that station and fire Ritz, she vowed. *That crusty bitch will still be there when I make my millions.* Ritz Harper would see Jamie again. And when she did, Jamie would be in control. She would have it all!

On Monday, Jamie reported to work. Before she could get situated at her workstation, she was given a pink slip. Jamie's first day of work was Skid Row Monday, the day the Dow Jones slumped nearly 780 points, marking the biggest single-day point loss in history. Jamie's new life was not to be. At least not yet. She knew she would have to move back home. And she would need another job.

Jamie called Ruffin.

8

Homicide detective Tom Pelov only trusted two things in this world: his Glock and his gut. And his gut was telling him that something wasn't right about the Ritz Harper case. Sure, it was closed, and he'd actually delivered the fatal bullet to the supposed killer. But something wasn't right. It was too neat. It was too perfect. There was more to this case. And Detective Pelov couldn't let it close.

Consider: Ritz Harper was a shock jock and a force in the music industry; the would-be killer, Jacob Reese (now deceased), was a music industry groupie, an aspiring producer. The music connection bugged Detective Pelov. Had Jacob been a crazed fan, or a murderous stalker, finding him scaling the fence at Ritz's home would be expected. But the music connection meant that something other than money was in it for him. Perhaps the promise of a record deal? If so, who promised it?

There were other problems: Jacob Reese was the kind of industry wannabe that nobody would have missed. He was expendable, and judging by the way he carried out his murder plot, Jacob was stupid, too. The music connection and Jacob's lowly status in the industry indicated that Jacob Reese was a hired gun. Killing Jacob before he got to Ritz was one small victory; but Jacob's employer was fully capable of hiring someone else to finish her off.

The irony, Detective Pelov knew, was that Jacob's fate was sealed the minute he took the job. Had he been successful in killing Ritz Harper, he would have become a dead man walking. Just three weeks before his retirement, Detective Pelov reopened the case. If his gut was right, Ritz Harper's would-be killer was still on the prowl. The shock jock had so many enemies, where would he start?

Detective Pelov emptied the contents of the Ritz Harper case file and studied his cast of characters. Next, he carefully read each statement gathered from the lone witness, and from friends and relatives who had gathered at the hospital for Ritz.

The old German/Italian detective grinned. "Holy shit." He laughed to himself. "Why didn't I notice this before?"

Detective Pelov tore one statement from the notebook and put a star on it.

"Gotcha!"

Ritz was ecstatic about the pitch meeting and especially excited that Chas actually had the juice to pull it off. She put on her game face for Ruff, anticipating his wrath when she asked for a few days off. Ruff was entitled to vent—Ritz was his star talent, and she had just got back in the swing of things.

Ritz strolled into Ruff's office and plopped down on his gray leather couch. Ruff was busy sending an e-mail to the Three Suits, a trio of wealthy white boys who had bought the station from the Gogel family. The Three Suits had requested the playlists for the week; they often asked for such mundane things. Asking for playlists, especially when they didn't know any of the urban songs on the lists, was just their way of exerting control. The hell with that the station was fiscally sound, operating underbudget, and had sky-high ratings; the Three Suits wanted Ruff to answer to them, to send the message that although Abigail Gogel strutted around the station as if she still owned the place, she really didn't.

Ruff looked up from the e-mail long enough to acknowledge Ritz. She'd interrupted his thoughts, as usual.

"Look, Ruff, I realize that I'm just getting back into my groove, after the baby and all—"

"It's not in the budget, Ritz," Ruff said, cutting her off. Whatever Ritz Harper wanted these days got a swift hell-to-the-nawl.

"Ruff, I'm not asking for a Macy's Day Parade."

"That's a first."

"Look, I want to take a few days off. I need to relax my mind, to do some searching to see what else the *Excursion* can become."

Ruff smiled broadly. He didn't know what her angle was, but getting her out of that studio right before the ratings report hit would be great for Michelle Davis. Ruff tried not to be too supportive of the idea. He didn't want her to know that he was desperate to cut her loose.

"Well, I do understand that you've been through your share of tragedy over the past few months," he said. "But I don't know. You have been away a lot over the last few years. I will run it by Abigail and see what she says. I'm sure she'll be fine with it, though. And what about Chas? Do you want him to stick around the studio, to work with one of your seat-warmers while you're gone?"

Ritz spun around like Linda Blair . . . all she needed was a mouthful of pea soup to kick off the *Exorcist* reenactment.

"No!" she roared. "Chas is going with me. We both need to reevaluate the show."

Ruff furrowed his brow. Her reaction was definitely out of order. But Ruff knew what Ritz meant, and he didn't care enough to warn her about the noncompete clause in her contract. He wanted to ship her ass to the competition. Ruff nodded and returned to his e-mail. This time he was sending a note to Michelle Davis: *It's time for you to work behind the mic again!* He was smiling.

Ritz stood up, her hands on her hips. "Well, aren't you gonna ask me where we're going and when we're coming back?" Ritz said, now curious about Ruff's reaction, which was out of the norm.

Ruff didn't even look up from the e-mail. "Be safe," he said halfheartedly.

As Ritz was leaving, Jamie was heading toward Ruff's office to thank him for the second chance (and the assignment change). Just in time she spotted Ritz leaving and ducked into an open space and waited for the six-foot siren to mosey on by.

"Fucking bitch," Jamie said under her breath. "Nasty. Ho. Bitch."

Jamie hated Ritz openly now. And she didn't care who knew. Ruff had assigned Jamie to Veronica Villagomez's show, the *V Spot*, and she was happy. Jamie had no reason to ever speak to Ritz.

Not that Ritz cared. Ritz would've thought nothing of speaking to Jamie, and she actually wanted to talk to her nowadays because Derek had vamped. He hadn't returned any of her calls, and his voice mail had been full for a week. Ritz didn't think that Derek would double-back to lame-ass Jamie, so she was concerned. And horny.

9

Chas would never acknowledge that outing so-called thug rappers resulted in high ratings, and for obvious reasons. The well-dressed cosmopolitan cutie enjoyed his fair share of down-low lovers, and Ritz's "Gay Fridays" segments severely limited his dating pool. No matter where her gay gossip came from, the public automatically assumed he was the source.

For this "Gay Friday," Ritz revisited an oldie but goodie, with even more dirt. Aaron played his intro, a two-snaps-up rendition of Donna Summer's "Bad Girls". . . *toot toot, hey, beep beep* . . . as Ritz reeled in her listeners.

"So, how you doin'?" Ritz purred.

The seemingly innocent phrase was the code intro for some tawdry gossip, and her audience knew it.

"Well, I've always been up front about who I bring home," she began. "I guess that gives me the liberty to point out the pillow-biters that want to pretend that they're not on the team.

"For those tuning in for the first time who may not be up to speed, let me school you on the gay studio thugs. I love the hotness. I love *honest gays*. And I love *closet gays*. It's the *studio gay-bashing thugs* that I'm outing. There are corporate conversions—these rappers and singers who sleep with recording industry types just to get a deal. But even after they get the deal, they still allow banji boys to tap them in the phatty. But artists, deejays, dancers, roadies, and label CEOs all play the thug role. Some play the role so well that they also have girlfriends and baby's mamas and they rap about killing down-low jiggas on their albums.

"Which brings me to today's 'Gay Friday' super star . . ."

Aaron cued up Diana Ross's hook, "I'm . . . coming . . . out . . . "

Ritz swiveled in her chair. She enjoyed this more than a ride at an amusement park. The Queen had been hinting all week about some explosive gossip that she couldn't wait to tell her league of loyal listeners. And now it was time to dish the dirt.

"I won't be too hard because I know Chas digs this

guy," Ritz teased. Even Chas's ears perked up. *What* was Ritz about to say?

"Well, here it goes. My sources tell me, and I've had three different sleuths to verify this, that Hardcore has been making the phatty-only party rounds.

"You remember Christopher Hardcore Harris, don't you? The multiplatinum rap artist, self-proclaimed hit man, and protégé of kingpin Tony Montana? Well, it seems Christopher has been working those lips again, and I don't mean spitting lyrics."

Aaron blasted one of his favorite sound effects, Ice Cube and Chris Tucker's "DAMMMMMNNNN . . ." from the comedy film *Friday*.

In Los Angeles, Christopher "Hardcore" Harris sat in his sparse mansion, the only remnant of his past riches. Ritz Harper had accused Hardcore of being a gay rapper and effectively ended his stellar career.

Almost immediately, Hardcore planned a comeback; and he would be so hard this time around, no one would ever believe the gay rumors.

Hardcore went underground, reinvented himself, and reemerged as the Dark Beast, a Goth-inspired rap artist.

No label would meet with him, so Hardcore took matters into his own hands. He filmed his own video and released his entire album on the Internet. He was confident that fans would support him.

The first release—which went straight to YouTube—was "Soul Stealin'," a sinister rap (with a hook from a nursery rhyme) that paid homage to grave robbing:

> *A tisket a tasket*
> *crack open that nigga's casket*
> *get the gold tooth out of that nigga's mouf*
> *he won't need it*
> *cuz he's gone down south*

The light-complexioned Dark Beast dusted his face with white, translucent Goth powder and encased his eyes in vamp eggplant eye shadow. He donned Victorian, black brocade trousers and high-heeled Goth gentleman's boots. With his full-length, three-tier coachman's cape, the Goth transformation was complete.

On the video shoot, Dark Beast was outside a graveyard, during daylight hours. He was so busy posing and lip-synching for the camera, Dark Beast didn't see the actual interment that was taking place behind him. (That family was now suing him.)

Hardcore anticipated the video to go viral, and it did, after *Vibe* trashed it: "Hardcore's ghoulish fake-Goth-star alter ego is the biggest marketing flop in the history of hip-hop."

Rolling Stone was worse: "Hardcore's career is dead and buried. Perhaps he should venture into the graveyard to dig that back up."

The video generated more than a million hits, but less than a hundred downloads of the album.

Not one to give up, Hardcore sent a demo to Goth rocker Marilyn Manson, seeking a rap duet. He was actually considering it. Things were looking up, Hardcore thought.

He was listening to the *Ritz Harper Excursion* and couldn't believe that she was outing him again!

Ritz continued, "The DownSouth crew, you know, those Atlanta gay boys, threw a backyard barbecue in a rented cabin. Hardcore was there, and my sources tell me that he disappeared into the back room, where he served it up real good. And the entrepreneur passed out his CDs, too! Hardcore might have thought that his salad-tossin' tongue tricks were safe, but the party hosts had cameras in every room to broadcast live footage throughout the cabin. The revolving door of DownSouth boys report that Hardcore is very talented, although everyone left their CDs behind."

The phones lit up.

"Hey, Ritz. This is Babydrinka from the Bronx, and let me say one thing, Ritz. I wanna get on that VIP list when Hardcore comes to town. His brain is fire!"

Ritz went to the next caller, a woman.

"I'm not surprised by the down-low parties anymore. But why not let us women hang around so that we can learn a few tricks?"

Ritz laughed at that. "Yeah, let's open a BJ academy! Let Professor Hardcore share his secrets."

Aaron played the sound of someone slurping a drink. Then a caller stopped him cold. Aaron mouthed to Chas, "It's Hardcore. Should I punch him through?"

Chas thought for half a second. "Yeah."

Aaron hesitated. "Are you going to tell Ritz?"

"Just put him through." This was going to be interesting. Ritz was oblivious, and that made for great radio moments.

"You're on the *Excursion,* speak your mind," Ritz said.

"Bitch, you're dead!" Click.

The caller's rage sent a chill up her spine.

"Dayum, dude, it's just radio!" Aaron yelped over Al Pacino's "Say hello to my little friend" clip from the film *Scarface.* "We play the hits, we don't deserve a hit."

Ritz was speechless.

Chas instructed Aaron to play the outro.

Ritz tried to regroup and signed off. "I will be away for a few days getting some Hollywood sun and some more dirt, so take care and I'll catch you back here on Wednesday!"

The ON AIR sign turned off and Ritz went off.

"How in the fuck did that happen?" she tore into Chas. "Did you want me to have a panic attack on the air?"

Chas was pleased. His poker face was solid. "Shock works both ways; it made for great radio, trust," said Chas, his delivery believable.

But Ritz was still angry. "Los Angeles will do us some good," Ritz huffed loud enough for everyone to hear. "I need to reevaluate a few things about you and me."

Hardcore didn't care about threatening Ritz on the air. His revenge mission had morphed into blind obsession, and thinking things through was not a part of the agenda.

Hardcore had tried to keep his hands clean by hiring someone else to off Ritz, but now he would handle this himself. She'd given him just the opening he needed: Chas, her right-hand man, was a fan. Hardcore only had bittersweet memories of the sunnier times, when his CDs were selling and he was rolling with his Uni-Global rep, Tracee. She was smart and spiritual, and she was Ritz's friend—allegedly. That was the part that really irked Hardcore: outing him made Tracee's career collateral damage and Ritz didn't give a fuck.

How poetic it would be to gun down New York's Queen of Radio in his own backyard. Hardcore examined his Jacob, an oversize diamond timepiece from a time when things were good. He intended to pawn it. He'd paid more than $200,000 for it. He hoped he could get at least $50,000 for it now.

How ironic that this was the second Jacob involved in the Ritz Harper murder plot. This Jacob would do its job, which was to fund the hit, unlike hit man Jacob Reese, who'd failed and got killed himself.

Hardcore prepared for his rendezvous with revenge. He finished his blunt, donned a black hoodie and baggy jeans. His next stop was the pawnshop, to trade the Jacob and buy a gun.

Hardcore missed one irony—his onetime manufactured murderous persona was now his reality.

At NYPD headquarters, Captain John Frankie, his trademark stale coconut doughnut in one hand, and a flask of whiskey and orange juice in the other, stopped by Detective Pelov's desk. In better days, Captain Frankie was a dead ringer for a young, *Braveheart*–era Mel Gibson. Nowadays, he was a dead ringer for an old Rolling Stones–era Keith Richards. The three divorces and five daughters had really sucked the life out of him. Appearances aside, Captain Frankie was still a solid cop.

"Pelov—that radio chick just got a death threat," the captain said, unknowingly spewing bits of coconut onto Pelov's desk. "It would be a shame for her to get popped before your retirement party. Put a car on her."

Detective Pelov agonized about how best to protect the deejay with the death wish. He was making progress, though, by narrowing his list of potential suspects to the outed celebrity and, possibly, the jilted insider.

10

Tracee's days at Uni-Global Music Group marked a bad time in her life and she didn't like discussing it. But with Randolph, she could, as he understood how important it was to leave the title and the money behind if staying meant selling out her soul.

And back then, she was doing exactly that.

The first time Ritz crossed her by outing her client Hardcore, Tracee wrote it off as a blessing in disguise. After his career tanked, Tracee gained clarity, and she didn't want to be a part of an industry that was so callous and cruel. Worse, Tracee knew Hardcore's true persona; he was a good guy from a bad situation and was doing things for himself. He didn't deserve Ritz's rant and the failure and ridicule that followed.

Ritz never apologized, really, and Tracee didn't feel she had to. Ritz had ratings to think about, and ratings begot wages.

But for Ritz to bring Hardcore up a second time? And provoke the man to call? Tracee was beside herself. Randolph had questions of his own about his newfound sister.

"Is money and fame that important to her?" Randolph asked. "Does she want to die over gossip?"

"I never understood it," Tracee said. "Trust me, the old Ritz wouldn't risk it all for money and status. Sometimes, I think of what she does and who she destroys in order to obtain the trappings of wealth, and it's frightening."

"*Trappings* is the right word. She is trapped. Trapped by the rat race of acquiring things, at any cost. It's more dangerous because someone tried to take her out before. I just don't want *you* to become the killer's next target."

Tracee's eyes grew wide. "Me? You don't think that someone would do that, do you?"

"Look, Ritz doesn't deal drugs. She isn't a gangbanger. All she does is gossip, and someone wanted to kill her over it. That person is demented, and you could definitely be a part of his scheme."

"But that detective killed the guy who shot Ritz."

"True. But now there's another one out to get her. You heard him on the radio, everybody did."

"I understand what you're saying and I appreciate you for not saying it outright, Randy."

He pulled Tracee closer to him; her head rested under his chin. He loved the smell of that lemon-meringue Miss Jessie's Curly Pudding that she used. She smelled like candy.

"No, Tracee. I *will* say it outright. We need to distance ourselves from Ritz Harper until this mess boils over."

"I can't do that," Tracee protested. "I love her. She's like a sister to me."

Randolph kissed her curly hair. "And I love you and I can't let my wife-to-be be in danger. I'm not having it."

Tracee looked up at him. "What did you just say?"

"I'm not having it!"

"No, before that."

Randolph smiled and crouched beside her on bended knee. He reached in his pocket and produced the famous aqua box with the crisp, white ribbon.

Tracee was shocked into tears. "Randy, Tiffany? Oh my God."

Tracee opened the box and marveled at the Tiffany Novo, two-carat engagement ring.

Randolph was a nervous wreck. "The salesman says that Tiffany, this ring is, um, pillow-cut."

Tracee corrected him, "Cushion-cut."

They laughed. She cried.

"That's right," he said, "cushion-cut, and that it was

created with fire and spirit. I'm an electrician, so I'm fire, in a way. And you have just brought this wonderful spirit into my life. Tracee, I don't want to scare you, but I've been going to Tiffany's and searching for your ring ever since the second time I saw you. Ask Emil, the salesman, he can verify . . ."

Tracee was speechless. Randolph took the ring out of the box and carefully placed it on her finger. It was a perfect fit.

"Tracee Remington, you bring out the best in me. I've always been a journeyman, looking for something solid, and you make me feel like home. No other woman could have guided me through this tough trial of losing respect for my dad, and finding a sister like that Ritz Harper."

They both laughed at that. Tracee still had tears from another place streaming down her face.

"Tracee . . . you are my fire, you are my spirit, and I am asking you, will you—"

Before Randolph could finish, Tracee jumped on him, sending them both to the floor. She kissed him all over his face, her tears and his tears becoming adhesive, and neither wanted to let go.

"Yes!" she said, sealing the deal. "I will be your wife. I will be your partner. I will be your helpmate. I will have your beautiful children."

Randolph was relieved. "And I will be in your corner. I will be your loving husband. I will be the best father, and the best friend to you . . . Mrs. Tracee Remington Jordan. I promise."

11

As an out-of-the-closet (but not flamboyant) gay man in the entertainment industry, and as the producer of the number one drive-time show in New York, Chas James's social calendar was something to behold.

There were always industry meet and greets, social mixers, club openings, launches, pre- and postparties, and Chas was on the VIP list for everything, no thanks to Ritz Harper, by the way.

Chas knew how to play the game. He understood that the ass you kick on the way up would be the ass you kiss on the way down. So he immediately smoothed things over with Ritz's furious guests. And Chas had a system. He'd work the celebrity's handler and say, "You know, Ritz just told the world that your client had herpes, but check the album sales tomorrow. Your client will thank her!" The handler and the dissed celebrity couldn't doubt that; any publicity was good publicity if it led to sales.

If that approach didn't work, Chas would give a wink to the dissed celebrity and promise, "As soon as you find some good dirt on that cow, I'll let you flip the script!"

That was a promise he could never keep, but it sure kept hope alive.

Chas was looking forward to this quick jaunt to L.A. Scores of beautiful gay men were in Los Angeles, but Chas only had eyes for one—Rutger Blake. Suddenly, someone just as enticing had eyes for Chas.

Aaron handed him the phone. "Hey, some dude says it's urgent."

Chas took the phone. "This is Chas."

"Look, man, I don't appreciate that shit." The meaty voice on the other end of the phone sent a chill down Chas's spine. Chas knew it was Hardcore. Ritz was right, Chas did have a thing for him.

"It's just showbiz, man," Chas said. "It's just radio."

"I feel like I need some reparations though, from you."

Chas's ears tweaked. "From me? How so?"

"You know what she's saying about me, and you don't even defend me. What's up with that?"

Chas laughed. Hardcore didn't sound too pissed now.

"I will definitely correct her next time," Chas said.

"You coming to my town, though? For real?"

The possibility of a hookup was so erotic that even the phone felt hot to Chas.

"Look, take this number and call me on my cell," Chas said. "I'll be leaving here in about five minutes. Let's talk about that."

Chas handed Aaron the phone and slipped out of the studio without telling the crew good-night. He was barely out of the studio when his cell vibrated. The area code was 310 and he knew what time it was.

"This is Chas."

"It's Hardcore. Look, man, I don't give a fuck about her, that shit's old. What I wanna do is, you know, grab a bite to eat or something when you get on the West Coast."

Hot damn! Chas's dick was dancing in his pants.

"How can I trust you won't beat me up?" Chas teased.

"I'm a lover, not a fighter," Hardcore spat back. "I'm just trying to settle a few curiosities that I have about you . . . if you can keep your mouth shut."

"I can," Chas said, trying to hold back his excitement, "for certain situations."

"Listen, I don't wanna keep bringing it up, but I want to see you, not an entourage. Just you. You understand what I'm getting at? No high-profile shit."

"Sounds like a plan." Chas blushed.

"We're on the same page. Trust."

12

Creepin' in Cali

Hardcore played roles well. In his former life, he was a studio gangsta. On this occasion he'd become a man-seducer. The role was tricky because Hardcore reasoned that "fags" were like bitches, except even more conniving. Hardcore had to watch his language. He had to pretend to be gay, although he wasn't gay, technically. Ramming some twink in a club that one time didn't make him gay. The twink wore lip gloss and fuchsia and was giving him that look. It was a club where secrets were made and kept, so why not? By this time, Hardcore had so much pussy on standby that trying something new was imminent.

But that was a long time ago. That was when he was trying to get into the game and his artist-and-repertoire handler told him that if he wanted his name to be considered for the more lucrative concerts, he should make the rounds at the DL industry parties. That's what Hardcore did, and from what he saw, that's what a lot of big names did, it was part of the hustle that would lead to a career.

Hooking up with Chas repulsed him. But he had to do it; he had to get to Ritz. And Chas seemed to be willing to lead him right to her.

In character, Hardcore placed the obligatory woo phone calls to Chas. He was especially careful to build Chas up as he tore Ritz down.

"I'm just saying, Chas, *you* have the talent," Hardcore said. "She's a talking head . . . with an awful weave!"

Chas soaked up every word and was thirsty for more.

"Chas, I'm sorry. I know you two are close. I guess I'm jealous, that's not gay, is it? Fuck it, then. I'll be gay for you. I'm jealous that she sees you so often and I gotta wait until you come through."

Chas was as giddy as a schoolgirl. And Hardcore couldn't believe how easy it was.

"I'd rather be with you, too. Trust," Hardcore said. "So where do you want to go when you get here? What can I treat you to? You know, that's discreet."

"How discreet do we need to be?" Chas asked.

"Ritz keeps putting the gaydar on me, and, Chas, if this was a booty call or something, I swear, I wouldn't care." Hardcore was putting it on thick. "But I dig you. I listen to the show because I know you're there working it behind the scenes, and I dig you. You know what? I wanted to ask you out that time I was on the show, but so much happened after Ritz blasted me. I couldn't dare take you out back and . . ."

"And what?" Chas teased. "Don't be shy."

"Cali niggas ain't shy, baby boy, not by a long shot. But I can show you better than I can tell you. So when are you getting here? When do we get some face time?"

"Soon. I'll text you when we leave New York."

13

The secluded eatery was serene and beautiful. Hardcore would have allowed himself to soak in the lush, floral Japanese garden and the warmth of the fireplace—if only the business at hand wasn't so ugly. Hardcore set the mood early.

"This is some weird shit, huh?" He smiled, flashing his flawless smile.

That smile was what hooked Chas the first time he saw him. Hardcore had great teeth. No jewelry or gang signs carved into them, which had become a trend in the industry. Hardcore's grill was just perfect, just like his large hands, and his gravel-deep voice, and his flawless butter-cream skin, with a tiny scar over his eyebrow.

Hardcore retrieved a tube of cherry Chap Stick and moisturized his lips. Chas was loving it. The servers set a bountiful array of colorful food on their table—bright orange sherry-vinegar and molasses-glazed carrots, spring-green broccolini and pecans, and a juicy, blackened rib roast with porcini stuffing.

"Enjoy," their lead server said.

"I will," Chas responded, eyeing Hardcore the entire time.

Hardcore managed a blush. "So, how long are you in town? What do you have going on?"

Chas told the plan without thinking twice. "We're meeting with the Big Four. Ritz wants to expand into television."

A pang of disgust struck Hardcore just as he swallowed his carrots. "What about you?" he recovered. "You're the one that needs to expand. No one wants to see her, you're the sunshine."

Chas smiled broadly. He could not believe this hunk was a gentleman. He loved such surprises. And the one-night-stand codespeak began.

Chas: "What do you wanna get into after this?" Translation: *Let's fuck!*

Hardcore: "I'm open to whatever." Translation: *Perhaps.*

Chas: "We should hang out at the Writer's Bar.

There are a few guys coming over to do spoken word, that's what the concierge told me. Last night, a few celebs stopped by." Translation: *Let's digest our food before we fuck!*

Hardcore: "On second thought, how about I allow you to unwind. You just flew in. And I have a few things I need to take care of back at my spot. We can hook up sometime tomorrow, after you're done with your business. You know, business is why you're here, right?" Translation: *I do not want any witnesses.*

Chas was deflated. But again, Hardcore was a gentleman, this could be the start of something more meaningful than Chas was accustomed to.

"That's cool, too," Chas said. "Jet lag is a mother. And I must be with that broke-down Queen of Radio tomorrow."

Hardcore leaned across the table and whispered, "I want you. I'm just confused and I want you in the right way. I want you to feel me when we're fucking and when you're on the plane going home. I wanna give you a reason to return. So, can we do that tomorrow?"

Chas nodded.

Hardcore summoned the server, peeled off three $100 bills, and slid them to Chas.

"This should cover us," he said, getting up from the table to reveal his rock-hard dick. "Take it as my down payment for tomorrow's session."

Chas couldn't wait to sleep with Ritz's enemy.

14

The Platinum Triangle, consisting of Bel Air, Beverly Hills, and Holmby Hills, was home to the priciest real estate in all of Los Angeles. Holmby, located on the cushy West Side, was the most exclusive neighborhood of the triangle. Rutger lived here among the rich and famous in the film industry.

Ritz entered the room and owned it.

Clad in a formfitting ensemble (rich, candy-apple red from head to toe), Ritz was a mesmerizing Monet, simultaneously regal and fierce.

"Wow," Rutger exclaimed.

His spontaneous reaction took Ritz by surprise, and she rewarded his candor with a warm smile. "I'm Ritz Harper," she said, beaming.

"Yes, you are, indeed."

Chas cleared his throat; Rutger should be fawning over him.

Rutger gawked at Ritz's legs, then shoes, then her waist, her soulful eyes, her impeccable long, flowing tresses; everything about this woman summoned his attention and he couldn't turn away.

Chas cleared his throat again, this time breaking the spell.

Rutger smiled at his favorite secret and hugged him head-on. "It's been so long, so very long since I've seen you, bloke."

Ritz smiled. Chas prattled on about the flight and the awful food, and Rutger was a most gracious host.

"Do you require a massage?" Rutger asked. "A bath? What would you like to eat? We can call in one of the best studio chefs, you'll be pleased."

Damn, Ritz thought to herself. Rutger didn't just dote on Chas, he spoiled him rotten. Chas responded to every generous gesture by batting his eyes and turning his chin upward. The more aloof he appeared, the more Rutger wanted to please him.

Ritz was beyond jealous. "Rutger, you have a lovely home."

"Thank you, Ritz. I try my best to make this place comfortable for me and my family. I go through so much in this industry, and I know I tend to bring it home to Ellie and the kids, so I want this to be a paradise for them."

"Oh, you're married?"

"Yes, my better half took the girls to the Atlantis resort in Dubai. Gretchen and Gabney bypassed Disney World for Alantis's Lost Chambers aquarium—it has a shark tank built into the wall."

"Really?" Ritz was impressed. "I love deep-sea creatures."

"Yes, my daughter Gabney wants to be a marine biologist so she's in fish heaven. I wanted to send her to Dubai before things got hot, if you know what I mean."

Ritz didn't know; but she pretended. "Your art collection is breathtaking."

Ritz stood there, long and shapely, with her hands on her hips. Chas had brought Rutger a new toy. And, boy, was she fascinating.

"Rutger has all but one piece of the Renoir collection," Chas boasted as he slipped his arm around Rutger's waist.

"That is true, and that bastard Jeremy Weinstein won't sell me *The Bathers* until ten years after his death. He's a prick."

"You have all the others, is it necessary to have that last painting?" Ritz asked.

Rutger crossed the room and led Ritz to the adjoining hallway to show his favorite piece.

"When I acquire *The Bathers,* the suite will be complete. And it will appreciate at lightning speed." Rutger winked.

"I appreciate it now," Ritz commented, totally missing the point.

Rutger smiled. He found her naïveté sexy. It exuded an innocence that was rarely found on his side of Hollywood—where everyone was so phony and always pretending to be more than he or she was.

Chas entered the hallway and watched with rage as Ritz studied the painting while Rutger was studying her frame.

"You know, Rutger," Chas said, "there was a time when I wanted to be an artist."

"Tell me about it."

Chas began to speak glowingly of his butterfly painting, something he'd created in grammar school. Ritz had heard this story many times before, so she ventured farther down the hall to view the other Renoirs.

The two men behaved like teens in love. Rutger threw his arm around the petite man and nuzzled his earlobe.

"That is fascinating," Rutger exclaimed. "So what would you need to resurrect that vision? Perhaps I could sponsor your adult art debut."

After endless chatter, Rutger invited Ritz to join him and Chas in the den. "Have a drink?"

Ritz declined. Chas attempted to pour his own, but

Rutger wouldn't allow it, saying, "You're my special guest."

Chas pointed to a bottle. Rutger dutifully handed Chas an elegant glass of bubbly.

"What do you know about Hollywood?" Rutger asked the two. "And don't be shy."

"I hear it's shady, hard to get in, but once you're in, you're in," Chas announced.

"What about you, Ritz? Are you familiar with the favor system?"

"Well," she stammered, "is it like the casting couch?"

"Yes and no," Rutger replied. "The favor system is not set in stone, there isn't an agreed upon give-and-take like with the casting couch. The favor system is a gamble. The giver wants to know just how low you will go to acquire his favor."

"Oh," Ritz said nervously. "We invented the favor system in radio."

Chas laughed at that. "But we are talking to the top dog, so that won't be a concern for you."

Rutger winked at Ritz.

She turned her head.

"But, hypothetically speaking, would you partici-pate in the favor system if you had to, Ritz?" Rutger asked.

Ritz held her tongue.

"I would, but only with you, bloke!" Chas joked.

Rutger turned to Ritz. "What is your limit?"

"What do you mean?"

"Okay, what is it exactly that you want to achieve on this visit?"

"I want a talk show. I want an opportunity to put the *Ritz Harper Excursion* on television."

Rutger inched closer to her. "Let's say that I'm the favor-giver who could bring that to fruition, but only if you were to sleep with me and my wife. Hypothetically speaking, of course. Would you?"

The suggestion struck a nerve. She said nothing.

"So tell me, Ritz, have you ever slept with a British bloke? My wife would make love to you for days. She finds the darker species so exciting. That's just one of the few things we have in common."

"I don't fuck for roles," Ritz shot back. "I don't fuck random white men, or their wives. That is one line that I do not cross. I fuck who I want to fuck just because I want to fuck them. And unless your wife is a big black man with a big black dick, I don't want anything to do with her, or you. Period."

Ritz rolled her eyes and ventured back into the hallway to get away from Rutger, who wasn't used to not getting exactly what he wanted.

Chas was stunned. If she wasn't willing to play the game, Rutger wasn't going to play either. Besides, he always followed his instinct about on-air personalities; within ten minutes he knew if an actor would connect with the audience—or not. This was golden for Rutger. This was bad news for Chas.

"Chas, I can't help her," Rutger blurted. "She isn't genuine. Her personality is just bad, from the first hello. Bad, bad, bad."

Chas couldn't argue with that and said, "But her listeners are devoted to her. She has a way with the people. Really, she's just nervous. That's all."

"Chas, nervous or not, her radio personality does not translate into an in-the-flesh warmth. Talk shows, of all media, rely on the strength of the host. She's not ready, not now. I can't help her."

"Rutger, why not? You've got more clout than anybody. You run this town!"

"I run this town, but I have the viewers to answer to. I can't put *that* on television—that woman has an ego of an A-list thespian—and a Q rating of a homeless person. No one knows her here. Throwing her on television just because I have the power to do so is the wrong thing to do in my position."

Chas paced the floor to alleviate that sinking feeling. If Ritz wasn't on the radar out here, that meant he was a nobody as well.

"What can we do to boost her Q rating?" Chas was desperate. "You know, if she makes it, so do I."

Rutger lowered his tone. "I can't manipulate Q ratings, not even for you. It's detailed research about how recognizable she is, and how well audiences respond to her. Ritz Harper has major strikes against her television debut. She's a radio shock jock, so she's heard but not seen; her 'royal' off-air persona is a turnoff; her

ego and demeanor are offensive. And she's a paid celebrity gossiper. That will never fly."

As much as it killed him to admit it, Chas knew
that he and Rutger were on the same page. Chas had
told Ritz to spend more time in the community with
her fans, but if it wasn't about money, she wanted
nothing to do with it. He warned her to treat those in
her camp better, but Ritz often mistook a worker's fear
of unemployment for loyalty, and she was a notorious
bitch. And Chas had encouraged Ritz to dress better,
of course, but now she outswaggered the queen of
England, which didn't vibe well with her minions.

But Rutger was wrong about gossip being a hin-
drance to Ritz's television debut, and Chas told him as
much: "Gossip drives the entertainment industry, and
Ritz is hot because she tells it like it is."

Rutger was dismissive. "Gossip is sausage for the
famished. People enjoy consuming it, but they want
nothing to do with the pig afterwards."

Chas had to laugh at that. *That bitch Ritz was a self-
ish pig.* He only wished she could have been in the
room to hear the comparison. Chas lowered himself
to the floor, on bended knee. This was his last-ditch ef-
fort to get the ball rolling for Ritz. He had to entice
Rutger.

"You know how adorable you are to me that way?"
Rutger smiled as he extended his hand. "Get up. I
would hate for Ritz to walk in on something that she's
not into. That would be interesting."

Chas obliged. "I promised Ritz that I could make

this happen because I know you," he told his old lover. "I am asking you to do all you can, so at least she knows that I tried."

With that, Chas planted a deep, wet kiss on Rutger's mouth, simultaneously massaging his throbbing dick with both hands. That's what Rutger loved about Chas, he never cared about keeping up appearances. Rutger pulled away from Chas, his blue eyes blazing with inspiration.

"Unless . . . ," he said, just as Ritz reentered the room, "my neighbor Ian could help. Let me make a call."

"What? I have to meet someone else now?" Ritz said in disgust. "Chas, does he even know who I am?"

Chas placed his finger to his mouth, motioning for Ritz to keep cool. Rutger whipped out his cell phone and crossed the room.

"Yes, Ian, it's Rutger. . . . I have a prospect, someone that could use your influence. She's far too green for the board to consider. Could I bother you with a pour? She and her producer are here for another day or so."

Chas awaited the verdict, but Ritz hit the roof.

"Who in the fuck is he calling green?" she fumed. "I am the number one host in all of fucking New York City. Chas, what the fuck?"

This time, Chas cut Ritz a look so vicious that words were not needed. Ritz fell in line, at least momentarily.

"Humph," Chas said under his breath as he moved

---

away from Ritz and closer to Rutger. Chas was still tripping about how Rutger knew Ritz so well after one brief meeting. And Chas was worried. Ritz was such a whiner; would she be "on" for meeting Ian on such short notice? She wasn't good without preparation, and with this last-minute arrangement Chas wasn't sure if Ritz would act right. Chas turned to Ritz to see if he could read her. Ritz, still pissed, managed a faint smile for Chas. He returned the love.

"You're a good man," Rutger said into the phone. He slipped it back into his pocket and shared the good news.

"I've arranged a small pour for you with Ian—"

"What's a pour?" Ritz butted in.

"Ritz, I apologize," Rutger said. "It's industry-speak for a casual get-together where quality liquor is served. Ian stays right up the way from here. He is someone that could help you out."

"So is this the pitch meeting?" Ritz queried. "If so, who are we meeting with and how can he help?"

"Ian Hale is a former studio executive who is now the chief of diversity initiatives for NAG, the New Actor's Guild."

"Diversity?!" Ritz blurted. "So I'm filling a quota now? Whatever."

Rutger ignored her and focused on Chas.

Chas was hopeful. "So Ian can open a few eyes for us?"

"More than that. Ian is the entryway to the small screen for unknown minority performers."

"So there is a quota," Ritz interjected. "That's funny. I thought that black celebrities paid their dues and competed for roles alongside everybody else. I didn't know there was a fast-track back door to stardom."

"Don't get it wrong," Rutger said sternly. "In 1999, a diversity study was issued, and none of the Big Four networks featured minority actresses in leading roles. It was a public relations disaster. Some contend that there were limited faces of color because the Screen Actor's Guild required at least two paid performance roles for membership; and if you're not a member of SAG, you can't work. So Ian stepped up to the plate and created NAG, the New Actors Guild. A one-year affiliation with NAG guaranteed an entrance into SAG, and into the industry. It's a program that we in Hollywood are very proud of."

"Rutger, does Ian know that I'm on WHOT?" Ritz asked. "Or that I'm syndicated in thirty states? I should be given a pass into SAG right away!"

Rutger no longer concealed his contempt. "Woman, radio does not make you an actor!"

"But I bring the drama in drive time! That's improv—four hours a day!"

"Bringing your radio drama does not make you a qualified talk-show host," Rutger said. "Chas, please take this celebrity to Ian, and let's see what he can do for her."

Ritz tapped her foot, but held her tongue.

Rutger approached her, staring directly into her eyes. "It is in your best interest to go with Ian's program. If you fuck up with him, you've fucked up with me."

"And then we're both fucked!" Chas joked, but not really.

Rutger smiled at his fuck buddy. "Never you, with a mouth like that. You should train Ritz on how to be quiet long enough for me to shove my cock in her mouth."

Ritz's mouth fell open. But the cuss words got lodged in her larynx. Chas laughed nervously but didn't like the insult one bit. He knew that within every joke was a half-truth. Did Rutger want to jump Ritz?

"Ian's home is four doors down on the left," Rutger said. "The walk will do her some good. Chas, come back and see me after you've dropped her off. We'll have dinner, and I'm certain we have much to discuss."

With that, Rutger walked out of the study.

"He couldn't get a fucking car for us?" Ritz complained as she and Chas clunked down the long, winding street. "I mean, what the fuck is his problem? These shoes cost me nine thousand dollars!"

"They're made for walking, right?"

"Oh, now you're getting on me, too?" Ritz huffed. "What did I do to you?"

Chas corrected himself. "Ritz, tone it down a bit.

Be a diva after you get what you want. Just, just, don't be so extra right now. We're going to meet with the diversity chief, and I want you to just be cool."

"I was cool when that motherfucker said that he was going to shove his dick in my mouth. I was cool when he kept referring to me as a nobody. I'm not a fucking nobody. If I'm a nobody, then you're a nobody, too!"

"Yeah, I know," Chas sulked.

In the distance, a white Mercedes sped toward them and hugged the curb at an unusually high speed.

"Oh, fuck!" Ritz screamed. She fell to the ground.

Chas turned to find Ritz on the ground in the fetal position, clutching her chest.

"Baby, what's the matter? What happened, Ritz?!"

Ritz was breathing hard, tears welling in her eyes. Chas fought to remove her hands from her chest. Was she bleeding? Ritz's heart was beating so hard, so fast, that it appeared to be bulging from her crimson dress.

"I'm okay," Ritz whispered. "I just thought . . . that someone had come back for me."

Chas placed his arms around her. "Don't panic. You're okay. You're okay. I'm right here. You know, we're far away from danger. Jacob Reese is dead. You're going to get your talk show, and you're going to get a change of scenery."

"Will you be with me, Chas? I don't have anybody."

"Yeah, you know that. We will have a change of scenery. Come on now, Ritz, get up."

Ritz didn't move.

"Come on, get up before you fuck up all that star shit you got on."

Ritz managed to laugh. Yeah, she didn't want to mess up her new dress.

"Do I look okay? Is my makeup fucked?"

Chas pulled a silk hankie out of his pocket. He stood on his tippy-toes and patted her concealer.

"You have the most beautiful eyes in the world, do you know that? You just trip people up with them."

Ritz smiled. Yeah, she knew her eyes were the prize.

"Okay, are we ready?" she asked.

"Yep. Let's keep it moving. And, Ritz, remember what Rutger said, go with Ian's program."

"I got it. I'm not leaving here without my talk show, Chas. You can believe that."

"Oh, I believe that." *Sort of.*

15

Friday, 10:15 p.m.
Holmby Hills, California
Ian Hale's mansion

Ian's redbrick, two-story mansion lay smack-dab in the middle between Rutger's home and the Hugh Hefner estate. With large windows, white columns, and a front porch with a swing, the home was an elegant, yet out-of-place, antebellum relic.

Chas rang the bell. In an instant, the New Yorkers stood face-to-face with an ebony-complexioned, portly, middle-aged woman. She was clad in a black-and-white housekeeper uniform with a matching head scarf.

"You've got to be fucking kidding me," Ritz mumbled.

"How you doin'?!" the housekeeper said to Ritz excitedly. Ritz returned a lukewarm "Hello," quickly followed by "Look at the throwback mammy," which she whispered to Chas. He didn't say a word.

The front porch led into an expansive entrance hall. Imported oil paintings and antique European furniture were among the visible symbols of Ian's wealth. To the left of the entranceway was a parlor, a dining room, and a sitting room. A grand winding staircase led to the upper-level master bedroom and guest quarters.

Ritz's eyes were drawn to a large, out-of-place mahogany display cabinet at the base of the winding stairs. Inside the cabinet was a collection of odd-looking drinking glasses, dolls, ashtrays, and postcards. She approached the cabinet and peered inside.

The soft voice of the housekeeper broke her concentration: "Ma'am, excuse me, Master Ian does not like anyone near his collectibles."

Chas and Ritz traded glances as Ritz mouthed, "Did she say *master* or *mister*?"

Chas shrugged his shoulders. "And what in the fuck is she wearing?" he said under his breath.

"It's called a uniform, sir," the housekeeper responded, startling them both. "Not everyone works in Hollywood, sir. Master Ian wants you to join him in the parlor. Follow me."

The house felt cold, despite the beauty and overall luxe, as if love never lived here. That feeling was cemented by the portly black housekeeper's greeting. Her words were polite, but her smile never reached her eyes.

"Ritz Harper," bellowed a pasty, stocky, bald, older man. He looked like a human egg, with red facial hair. "I've heard of you."

"You have?" she said, thinking, *Finally someone has heard of me.*

"Of course I know of you. As diversity czar, it's my duty to know what's going on in the street."

Chas extended his hand, but Ian gave him a big hug instead.

"I'm sure Rutger is expecting you to return," Ian said. "It was great to meet you."

The housekeeper approached and seemed eager to put Chas out.

"Ritz will join you later," Ian added.

"Yeah, I was a little concerned," Chas protested, albeit less like a man, and more like a mouse. "We came together; I thought we would leave together."

Ritz said nothing.

"Just because you're both here at the same time doesn't mean you're together," Ian said with a chuckle. "Together implies a partnership, on some level. So, Ritz, are you together? Would you care to stay with me or leave with Chas?"

Ritz winked at Chas. "I will stay with you, Ian. I already know what Chas is working with!"

They all laughed. Chas kissed Ritz on the cheek

and whispered in her ear, "Don't worry. Just play the game. Play the game."

Chas shook Ian's hand and exited with the housekeeper. The two paused at the door.

Chas turned to the housekeeper before leaving. "How can you wear that? It's so degrading."

The housekeeper adjusted her head scarf. This time she flashed a genuine smile. "I know many guests have wanted to ask me that, but they never have. Since you asked, I'll tell you the truth. I'm playing a role. Master Ian wants a mammy type to dust and answer the door. He's got it. I want a six-figure income for doing next to nothing, and I've got it."

Chas shook his head in disgust.

The housekeeper unlatched the door, but did not open it. "I would ask you how could you work for her because she's degrading you. But I know you don't have the answer."

"What?"

"Sir, you don't even know who she really is. That's why you're still shocked that you're leaving here alone."

She opened the door to the speechless Chas and said, "Good-bye."

"Have a drink with me, Ritz?"

"Sure, Ian. Do you have champagne, Georges Vesselle?"

He laughed. "How about some genuine one-hundred-and-ninety-proof corn liquor? Some genuine Confederate truth serum."

Ian winked as he poured a short glass of clear liquid and handed it to her. "This is a neutral concoction—tasteless, odorless, but quite effective."

Ritz held the glass to her nose and winced. She babysat the drink.

"Go on, splash your tonsils!"

"You know, Ian, I haven't eaten dinner, and, um, I don't want to start with this. I don't need the truth serum. I'll tell the truth, if you do."

"Fair enough. My credentials don't make good conversation. I prefer personal questions, if you don't mind."

"Are you going to dictate what I ask, or do I have some control, Ian?"

"You can have some control. For now."

"What's behind your passion for diversity?"

Ian threw the corn liquor down his throat. He swished, swallowed hard, then wiped his mouth with the back of his hand and poured himself another.

"I do this to pay homage to my parents," he said.

"Really? Tell me about it."

"My mother was a homemaker. My grandfather was a surgeon, and he wanted that for my father. He told my father that if he didn't go to med school, he would be cut out of the will. So my father did what every young man does when given an ultimatum to go to med school."

"And what's that?" Ritz smiled.

"He pursued exactly the opposite—he studied special effects."

"Special effects? Wow. That must have been interesting for a young boy."

"Yeah, it was pretty fantastic," Ian said. "He built creatures and created deformities for many of the early horror films. He made a lot of money in this town. Hale was a good name then."

Ian took a swig of the corn liquor. He confiscated Ritz's glass.

"You really should have taken your truth serum. It'll come in handy later." He laughed.

"So, how did this lead to your passion for diversity?"

The red-faced man closed his eyes and revisited the past. "My father started his company in the garage of our home. He went around everywhere, hustling those little monster dolls, to theme parties, to circuses, anywhere there was a group of people with money to spend. And then Warner Bros. called. My father was making movies, he was a big shot. We bought this house. My father would bring rejected prototypes home for me to play with."

Ian paused. He glared at Ritz—she could have sworn that the room temperature had dipped ten degrees. He poured another drink.

"And then . . . I left one of the toys on the stairs. My mother slipped on it and fell down the stairs and twisted her spine like a pretzel. Her legs were useless. My father hired Ms. Natalie to care for my mother."

Ian threw the glass across the room. Ritz jumped as specks of shattered glass landed at her feet. "That was the first time I ever laid my eyes on a nigger woman."

"What did you say?" Ritz was incredulous.

"Ms. Natalie, oh, she was so good at cleaning up after us. She was so good at cooking dinner for us. And she really wanted to be my mother. She was so good at seducing my father and me. My father was weak; that nigger mesmerized him. He made dolls in her likeness. He took photos of her and pinned those photos on these very walls.

"Ms. Natalie had me in a trance, too. We had great times. She was like a mother to me. My mother would call for me and I'd ignore her. I would hide. I was so young, I was six years old. What kid wants to sit in his mother's room? I wanted to play in the yard with Ms. Natalie. Me and my father neglected my mother. We wanted Ms. Natalie."

"You were just a child, Ian," Ritz tried to comfort him.

"One night I heard my mother sobbing. That's the worst sound a son could ever hear, his mother sobbing. Everything was my fault. I left my toy on the stairs. I broke her body. I brought that whore in this house. That time she called for me I obeyed. My mother told me to help her out of bed because she wanted to see the sunrise.

"I wanted to do the right thing. I wanted to do right by her. We were doing so well at first. I remember holding my arms out to catch her as she rolled out of bed. She fell and landed on top of me. Her legs were jelly and she was so heavy. But she was laughing. She was so happy to be out of that bed."

Ian's eyes grew wild. He was in the moment, stretching out his arms.

"My mother dragged herself across the floor and stopped at the top of the stairs. She told me to run, go get my father, let's show him the surprise. I ran into his study, but he wasn't there. He wasn't on the back porch either. He wasn't where he usually was, so I went into Ms. Natalie's room, and that's where I found them.

"They were naked and yelling at me: I should have knocked. I was a bad boy.

"That's when we heard the screams, the horrible crash of flesh and bone tossing about every other stair. I ran after my mother, but my father grabbed my shirt. I wasn't there to hold out my arms. I wasn't there to catch her."

"Oh my God, Ian, I am so sorry."

"My mother was so mangled and bloody. Some nights I swear I can still see her shaking at the base of the stairs. My grandparents cremated her. Too many injuries for an open casket."

Ian faced Ritz. "My father ran off with Ms. Natalie and didn't come to the funeral. I asked my grand-mother, 'Why would my father leave me? Why would she take my dad?' My grandmother told me, 'That's what niggers do. They take things that don't belong to them. Even men.'

"That's what you do," he said to Ritz.

Ritz ignored the insult. Instead, she focused on the hurt behind it. "What happened to your father?"

"He was dead two years later, a massive stroke. Probably eating all that soul food. He left the bulk of his fortune to Ms. Natalie and their mutt children. She didn't want this death house. Thank goodness for my grandfather's estate or I would have been a penniless orphan."

Ian's forehead was slick with sweat. "So I do what I do in honor of my mother. A nigger broke up her home, destroyed her marriage. Destroyed our family. So diversity is important to me. I want to roll out the red carpet so you can get everything you're due."

Ritz shifted her body away from him. "You want to help blacks in this industry because of what Ms. Natalie did to you?" Ritz was puzzled. "Does this give you closure? I don't understand."

Ian ignored her.

Ritz scanned the room for the nearest exit or, if it came to that, a makeshift weapon. "Ian, I think you've had too much to drink."

"If I make you uncomfortable, you can walk," he seethed. "You could walk, without your contract."

The threat was effective.

"It's a sad day when a white man is no longer in control of himself," he spat. "You voodoo bitches . . . you're unnatural."

"I don't like this conversation, Ian, and I'm not going to tolerate this shit."

Ian squeezed Ritz's hand and pulled her near. "You came here for something. You tolerate what I tell you to tolerate, or you'll leave without it."

Ritz wiggled free of his clammy grasp. "Ian, I have boundaries."

"If that's the case, you should leave now."

16

The Walk

The walk back to Rutger's house seemed to take forever. Chas's mind was reeling from the beautiful surroundings. The luxurious homes reminded him of what he did not have. The future, his future, rested heavily on what Ritz did in that house. And what did Ian want with Ritz? What was happening? Was she cutting a lucrative deal for herself only? Would she play the game? What was the game, anyway?

Chas wondered if Ritz could make it in Hollywood. And he wondered if he could make it in Hollywood with Ritz. Or were they both being delusional now?

Chas walked even slower, as if his shoes were filled with lead.

Chas knew the power of delusion—for years, he'd convinced himself of a future with that ruthless Rutger. For years, he'd promised himself that he would never return to the elusive lover who hurt him so.

Rutger was the first man ever to touch Chas; and to make love to him.

Prior to Rutger, Chas was the typical closeted black college kid, curious but fearful of the community's backlash.

Yet he yearned for men.

He stared at his male roommate, Leonard, as he slept.

He fantasized about Leonard's teammates. He jacked off to thoughts of spooning with his English professor.

Chas enrolled in mass-communication classes with an emphasis on sports production so that he could work with the football coach to tape the games. Chas wanted to be near Leonard to eavesdrop on him as he talked about fucking the easy girls. Chas imagined Leonard was fucking him.

During his junior year, Chas realized that sports production overwhelmingly placed him with straight jock clients, and thus he switched gears to entertainment production, with an emphasis on radio. In the wild world of music, the pickings would be more plentiful.

In 1999, Rutger and his girlfriend Ellie, two ivory-white, twentysomething jet-setters, arrived in New York City to catch a Broadway show and to bring in the New Year and, as many had erroneously thought, the New Millennium in Times Square.

At a quarter to midnight Rutger and Ellie would meet Chas and Leonard.

Chas and Leonard—Chas's unsuspecting crush—were also in Times Square standing shoulder to shoulder with the Brits. Chas had a few beers, readying himself to accidentally cup Leonard's ass when the ball dropped. What if Y2K did bring about the end of the world? Would Chas want to go out without having touched Leonard's ass?

Chas was nervous, and the churning beer in his belly was making him queasy. Still, Chas couldn't stop watching him.

Ellie couldn't stop watching Leonard either.

The tall, cinnamon jock with the broad football shoulders and the thick, wavy hair was making her blond pussy pulse with desire. Ellie envisioned Leonard breaking into their hotel room and tearing at her panties as Rutger slept.

Ellie and Rutger had mentioned doing something naughty to bring in the new millennium. So why not?

Rutger was feeling a pang in his loins; he wanted Chas and he didn't seek Ellie's permission.

Rutger leaned into Chas and made small talk. "You blokes know how to throw a party."

Rutger's thick British accent, sweetened by liquor, caused Chas's manhood to rise. Chas turned around and was mesmerized by the lean, dirty-blond six-footer. Rutger's dimpled chin and clear blue eyes were equally hypnotic as his sinister grin.

Rutger was drunk off his ass, but perceptive. "You should take a picture of your friend's bum, it lasts longer."

"Huh?" Chas was mortified. Good thing Leonard was too dumb to know that *bum* is Brit-speak for "ass."

Anyway, Leonard is distracted by Ellie, who stealthily offered him a blow job. "You know we can do it better, right, bloke?" she whispered in his ear. "You should join us."

Leonard was speechless.

Rutger threw his arms around the handsome men and asked them to show "the drunk Britons to their hotel."

Chas and Leonard are in the Hilton hotel suite, awaiting room service. Rutger's in the shower; Ellie is raiding the minibar. She removes a miniature bottle of Jack Daniel's.

She hands the bottle to Leonard. "Sprinkle your privates . . . I'm thirsty."

Chas's eyes grow wide, awaiting the reveal of Leonard's dick, finally.

That would have to wait, though. Leonard is upstaged by Rutger, who enters the room stark white and naked.

Rutger walks over to Chas, his soft dick swinging. "So, have you ever had a white one?"

"Huh?" Chas is too aroused to deny the gay rumors. Leonard's eyes roll to the back of his head as Ellie puts her hot, wet mouth all over his dick.

She pauses. "Join me honey. This Jack on black tastes supreme!"

Rutger lowers himself to his knees. He places one hand on Chas's thigh as he leans over and eases his mouth onto Leonard's dick.

The suckling and moaning echo throughout the room.

Leonard feels two mouths sucking on him and his eyes snap open. He glances at Chas.

Chas is watching Rutger take long, strong draws of Leonard's dick.

Leonard's and Chas's eyes meet, and Leonard doesn't protest. He places his hands on top of Ellie's and Rutger's heads and allows them to devour him.

Rutger's strong hand travels into Chas's zipper. Chas lowers his pants and underwear. He allows his knees to fall in opposite directions. "I want some," Chas murmurs.

Ellie stops sucking on Leonard and approaches Chas. "No," Chas says. "I want some of him."

Rutger led Chas to the unmade bed. He tongue-kissed him, then instructed Chas to lie on his belly.

Rutger massaged his dick with lubricant and lay on top of Chas. He situated his dick to caress—and then enter—Chas's virgin asshole.

"Bear down on me," Rutger told him. "Come on. It'll only hurt a little bit and then you'll be addicted to me." Chas arched his back and allowed Rutger to go deeper.

Ellie and Leonard joined the two on the bed.

Rutger's gyrating white body on top of Chas's beautiful brown body drove Ellie wild. She was uninhibited as she sucked and fucked Leonard.

Fully inside, Rutger gently pushed Chas's face into the pillow to muffle the moans. The once timid Chas was now pumping back, intoxicated by the mix of pleasure and pain.

Chas never imagined that a white man's warm cum would one day seep from his ass.

And he certainly never imagined that Rutger and Leonard would simultaneously suck his dick once it was over.

But it happened.

Chas and Leonard would have meaningless sex play sparingly after that day, but Chas longed for Rutger.

Six months after the one-night stand, Rutger came to New York to participate in a summer film program.

With Rutger at his side, Chas had grown comfortable with his true identity as a gay black man who loved a foreign white man.

Chas fell madly in love with Rutger and planned to be a longtime lover and helpmate to the future film-maker.

To celebrate the end of the summer film program, Chas and Rutger tipped a New York cabbie $100 to film them making love in the back of his cab.

Rutger promised Chas that he would apply for a visa and permanently relocate to the States, as soon as he got his business in order back at home.

Chas pined for Rutger, but didn't hear from him.

Days went by. Then weeks. Then a full year.

Chas repeatedly watched the cabbie sex tape—one frame in particular where Rutger, deep in the throes of the "best blow job" he's ever had, says to Chas, "I only wish . . . ," but doesn't finish the thought and he collapses in ecstasy instead.

As Chas watched the tape, he completed Rutger's thought on his on:

"I only wish I could . . . stay. I only wish I could . . . have you longer. I only wish I could . . . marry you and bring you to England."

Sixteen months later, Chas turned on the Emmys and saw Rutger and Ellie on the red carpet. They were in Los Angeles. Rutger was looking successful and well fucked. Ellie was sporting a diamond ring and a very pregnant physique.

Chas was devastated.

Chas called Rutger's studio in L.A. and demanded a meeting.

Rutger obliged and sent for him.

A car picked Chas up from his home and escorted him to La Guardia. When Chas arrived at Los Angeles Airport (LAX), another car whisked him away to Orange County, a popular neighborhood of the old-money set and the new-money set that weren't eager to flaunt.

Chas wanted to freshen up prior to his confrontation with Rutger, but no hotel plans were on his itinerary. Chas was to meet Rutger at the exquisite Rancho Las Lomas, a private zoological garden and popular wedding venue.

Rutger was as sly as the devil. Of course he would arrange to fight against the backdrop of cool reflecting pools, English rose gardens, and baby Bengal tigers.

Who could be angry in the midst of such beauty?

The driver helped Chas retrieve his things just as Rutger walked up.

"You might as well send the luggage back to New York," he mused. "You won't need clothes here."

Rutger had rented the entire estate for his lover, and they roamed the grounds wearing next to nothing. Chas never had the will to say no to the first man that ever touched him. But he didn't fly all the way from New York to get laid. Chas demanded answers.

"I waited for you, Rutger."

"I couldn't return to you."

"Those six months in New York were liberating for

me. How could you lure me out of the closet only to go in yourself?"

"I enjoyed every moment I spent with you, Chas. But I was only good for our moments. Your body, your jaws of life. You are the most fascinating human I've ever met."

"You knew that you were returning to her—"

"Chas, *no*. I never left her. She is dinner. You're dessert."

"So that's what I am, just your dark meat on the side?"

"When we are together, do you ever feel that way?"

"No."

"That's our moment. Hold on to it. Enjoy it when we're in it."

"I love you, Rutger."

"I'm married."

"I want to be with you."

"I'm a family man now."

"I know that you love me, too."

"I appreciate our moments. Fuck that, I crave our moments, Chas."

"We need to stop pretending."

"I would be pretending if I were to enter something more with you. The fact is, I'm not gay."

"Your dick seems to think so."

"You arouse me in ways that she never could. But I can't mentally, wholeheartedly, fall in love with a man."

"It happens every day of the week, Rutger."

"It won't happen between us. I'm sorry to have misled you. I thought that as a man, you could compartmentalize as a man. I thought you would understand the concept of moments."

"Like the rest of your bitches?"

"No, Chas, do not attack the women I sleep with. They are less than moments to me; they are a necessary evil in this town. Focus on our moments and nothing else. Things will be fine, I promise you."

And there it was: Chas could be content sleeping with the love of his life who didn't want him, or he could run away.

"Come on in, bloke!" Rutger said now from the entranceway of his home, breaking Chas out of his trance. "I've been waiting."

17

Playing the Game

Chas's parting advice, "Play the game," bounced around in Ritz's head. But if this was the kind of game she thought it might be, it was the one game she had promised herself that she would never play. Ritz's heart was pounding. Trickery was one thing, tricking off was another.

With Chas gone, Ian was ready to unleash his full agenda. Ritz looked spent. And she was. What had she got herself into? Here she was chasing dreams in California and risking her career back at home. A change of venue was good, but would she always double over in fear at the sight of a speeding vehicle? If so, the tabloids would have a field day with her.

Not that she had to worry about tabloids.

What bothered Ritz more than anything about L.A. was that no one, not the staff at the hotel, not at the spa, not passersby, no one, recognized her—and she was a star on the East Coast, and in thirty other states! And now she was sitting in a strange man's home hoping to get a crack at her television show just because she was black? Ritz Harper had been reduced to playing the race card from the bottom of the deck.

"Penny for your thoughts," Ian chided. "Tell me what's on that mind of yours."

"I want to know if you can really help me," she spoke clearly. "Something tells me that I am going to give up much more than I get tonight."

"Oh." He laughed. "I make the deals happen—but for a price that very few are willing to pay. Look at my Wall of Fame. Those are the women who have sat in the same seat you're sitting in now. Ritz, that is my prized collection. Most people see autographs, I see souls. I have keen memories of each smile. Recognize any of them?"

Of course she did. Ritz's mouth nearly crashed through the floor as she scanned the photo wall of black and brown celebrities, each with glistening white smiles and flawless airbrushed skin. Each autograph displayed a scribbled message of gratitude. She wanted to add her photo to the wall. But what would it take?

"So Rutger tells me that you want to host your own talk show," Ian said. "What can you add to the body of talk show entertainment?"

Ritz imagined that she was back in the studio behind the mic. In control. In command.

"I don't know if we, my demographic, can rely on what's out there to tell our stories. Some hosts are female or have brown faces, but they are giving us their limited life experiences. I'd like to see someone focus on our progressive, multicultural, hip-hop-meets-high-society stories. So far, no one is doing that."

"Great concept, but you're the wrong person to see it through," he said dismissively.

"What?" Ritz fumed. "How is that?"

"For one, you can promote multicultural all you want, but everything about you, from your European weave to your French manicure, screams that you want to assimilate into *my* culture, not celebrate your own."

Ritz was in disbelief. "You're so wrong. I like a little glamour, but I also love who I am."

Ian stroked the stubble on his bulbous face. "You women know how to speak your minds," he said with a smile. "And I like honest, frank conversation. Do you?"

"Yes, that's what I do every day. I talk honestly about whatever."

"Ritz Harper, I want to talk honestly about you. Tell me about yourself right now, in this very moment."

"I'm the Queen of Radio in New York, and I want

to conquer television," she said boldly. "I have a lot to say and I think that the world would embrace me."

"I've seen you a gazillion times," he chuckled.

"You've seen me?"

"Not you, per se, but your type. Every Jezebel whore, aspiring actress, or out-of-work reality star wants to be the next talk show queen. I've heard that line before and it tells me nothing about you. I want to know about you, in this very moment. Why are you here?"

Ritz bit her tongue and chose her words carefully. "I'm here because I want to take my radio show to television. I want to take my career and my audience to the next level."

"There you are, speaking of your career again. Let me tell you this up front. If you do what I ask of you, you will get your shot at a TV show. All I ask now is that you stop pitching and converse with me."

Ritz felt a wave of relief—she couldn't fuck this up, especially when all she had to do was talk. She took a deep breath.

"I'll answer your questions."

"Okay. Go stand on that platform over there and tell me about your outfit. It *is* fabulous."

Ritz rose from her seat and walked to the platform as if she were on a runway.

"Crimson and cream silk patchwork dress," she said, moving her hand over the fabric to display its beauty.

"And who is the designer?"

This one is easy. Ritz smiled. "Christian LaCroix Couture."

"And the hat?"

"A simple cherry hat, from Chanel."

"Ritz, those are the most beautiful shoes. Like art for the feet."

"Red snake . . . John Galliano for Christian Dior."

"Fabulous! Ritz, did you wear those big designer labels just for me?"

"Actually no," Ritz blurted. "I didn't even know about you until today. I work hard. I like nice things. I wear my star shit all the time."

"Must all nice things be so high-end?"

"I think most nice things are pricey."

"What do your clothes say about you, Ritz?"

Ritz looked down at her outfit. She had never pondered that question before.

"Confident. Classy. Well-dressed. Red says I'm outgoing . . . and fierce."

Ian chuckled again, this time it sounded more like the kind of laugh you would hear from the villain of a horror film.

"I'm sure that's what your homeboys in New York would think. Your outfit conveys the opposite to men of my caliber."

"What?"

"Foolish woman," Ian said bluntly. "The bigger the label, the smaller the person behind it."

"Um, no disrespect, but you don't strike me as one who is really into fashion. Trust me on this, image is everything."

"Yes, yes!" Ian said excitedly. "Image is key to *your* people. That's the fundamental difference between your people and my people. You are concerned with image. We are concerned with reality. See, you're dressed in big fancy labels, looking like a walking Times Square. Your image is great. But the reality is that I can buy and sell your ass ten, maybe a hundred times, and I'm wearing khakis and Birkenstocks."

Ritz bit her tongue so hard that she tasted blood. *Play the game,* she kept repeating to herself.

"You can step down from the auction block now," Ian said. "Do you like it? It's a family heirloom."

Ritz didn't quite process what he had said. She was still reeling from his previous statement.

"What are you proud of, Ritz?"

"Women are expected to fuck around to get ahead. Personally, I haven't slept with anybody for a job or a handout. That's what I'm most proud about. I worked hard to get to where I am, and I never had to compromise myself to do it. And I never will."

"You'd be surprised by what you would do, if given the right stimulation."

Ritz clenched her teeth, making her jawbone jut out just a bit. "I took the cards that I'd been dealt and I made something out of myself."

"You have made something of yourself. I'd like to

really see it, though. Please, convince me that you're worthy of a talk show. You're all dolled-up and you're still so basic."

"There's nothing basic about me. Name another woman who went through what I did and still managed to come back on top of the game. I have my life back and under control. I am in control. And I'm here, working on my next move, just like I wanted to do."

"Career is all you have. It is all you speak of!" Ian said just below a shout. "And you are not in control. You are not in control of the hot gossip that Chas brings to you. You are not in control of your ratings. You are not in control of aging. You are not in control of the men that roam in and out of your life. You are not in control of the baby that died in your arms or the bullets that invaded your flesh. You are not in control of anything! You have no reason to be proud."

"I can control this conversation!" Ritz exclaimed. "I don't want to have it any longer."

"I'm sorry," Ian said coldly. "If this makes you uncomfortable, you can always walk."

"I don't want to play this game. I don't know what you're expecting me to say."

"You've failed, Ritz, if this is how you are going to host your talk show. When a guest says something that you don't agree with, you're going to take the mic and go home?"

"No."

"It's this sense of entitlement that I smell about you. You stink of it." He walked closer to her, smiling. "Black women are especially intriguing to me. So passionate and strong. You're like roaches, you're cursed and crushed, but you never go away."

"What?! Ian, you're adept at delivering the backhanded compliment; something sweet, something shitty."

"Hollywood is up to its hairline in little black roaches," he said, dismissing her last statement. "You all think you're entitled to be the next It girl. And you just keep coming, although there are no quality roles for you. Audiences barely want to see you. Ninety-seven percent of you remain unemployed after your so-called breakthrough role. And you try so hard. How pathetic."

"Why must you compare us to roaches? Roaches are not generally considered strong . . . they're pests."

"Because you're the only species that survives with nothing and for naught."

"I don't agree. Everything I've wanted, I've gotten. I've had it all."

"What do you have? A great career? You work a job and you have no natural allies. You can't confide in white women, as they may be racist. You can't seek guidance from black men, as they are so busy bonding with white men that they become sexist toward you. There is no black female bonding because of your competitive nature, and no one sabotages a black woman the way that another black woman does. You have no mentors. You have no companionship nor any camaraderie. You work for cars and clothes.

"You have no one who has your back in the workplace, and it is this disconnect that makes black women excellent managers. Your loyalties lie with the only thing you truly trust—your work. And that's just one facet of your pathetic nothing of a life."

"That is not true! You've been misinformed."

"Really?" Ian said playfully. "Who will correct me, your invisible man? The only man in your life acts like a girl. Where is your husband or even a faithful boyfriend? But, yes, you know your situation better than I do. Enlighten me if I'm wrong."

He wasn't wrong. Ritz was silent.

"What we are doing here is reaching your core. Who are you, Ritz Harper, without the job and the jewels?"

She didn't answer.

"You're nothing! So humble yourself and behave like someone with nothing. Be nothing for a few hours and you'll have a shot at your talk show."

Ritz swallowed hard; the lump building in her throat felt the size of a grapefruit. She couldn't cry, not in front of this man. But he had hit a nerve. He more than hit it, he all but severed it. Ritz wished that he had so that she would not feel any of the pain.

"I don't know how to be nothing," she managed out of her constricted throat.

"Come with me, Ritz," Ian said warmly. "I can show you."

Ian led Ritz onto his sunporch in the back of his mansion. It overlooked two acres of lush greenery beneath a huge blue moon. Ian eased behind Ritz and slipped his cold, clammy hands around her waist.

Ritz jumped but didn't move away. It won't get that far, she told herself. He stood on his tippy-toes to talk into her earlobe.

"Do you know what that is?" he said, pointing out into what seemed like a mile of greenery. "You should."

"I don't know."

"It's my symbolic garden. Whenever I feel that we are losing the race of all races, I come back here and soak up the history, the beauty of what this field represents. I imagine a return to those good old days."

Ritz gently removed his hands from her waist and turned to face him.

"Ian, what are you growing back here?" she asked, but somewhere inside she knew the answer.

"Upland cotton," Ian said broadly. "I believe in history. I am an advocate of active history. I believe that history runs in our veins. We should map our future around it. You uppity niggers are out of control."

"What the fuck? Who the fuck do you think you're talking to like that?!"

"Nobody," Ian said, grinning.

Ritz was flummoxed. "And you're supposed to be some head of diversity?!"

"How else can I lure you nigger bitches here? Image is everything, right? Would you stop by if I had a cross burning in the front yard?"

"How could you?"

"Oh, I'm sorry. If I'm making you uncomfortable, you can always walk."

The floodgate was open now. The fury, the hurt, and the totally helpless converged and Ritz's tears wouldn't stop. "You are so wrong."

"Look, Ritz, that's a cotton field. You should know what that is. You niggers have been picking it for-ever."

The real Ritz Harper would have had three layers of Ian's flabby white skin under her nails by now. But she couldn't move. She couldn't say a word. She did nothing. *Play the game.* But what kind of game was he playing? Was Ian just trying to see how far he could go to make Ritz snap and leave? Well, he'd have to do better than that.

Ian's eyes were on fire. He was in his element. "Do you know your history?"

"I can only go back so far," said Ritz, composing herself. "My father hasn't been a part of my life, so there's a lot that I don't know."

Tiny beads of sweat dotted Ian's forehead. He was an animal on the prowl.

"Do you know the history of white men and black women?" he asked, circling Ritz. "Do you? How can you relate to me if you don't know our history?"

Ritz transported her mind, praying that her body would soon follow.

"Somewhat."

"Enlighten me, Ritz Harper. Tell me what you know."

"I know there were relationships that . . ." Ritz's voice trailed off.

"Tell me what you know, girl. Come on, tell me!"

"That when black women were slaves—"

Ian cut her off. "When *you* were a slave . . ."

"When my ancestors were slaves . . . that the slave master would have sex with them. Or, like Strom Thurmond, have families with them."

Ian stopped circling. "I love it when you women do that."

"Do what?"

"Try to clean up what happened. Pretend that there was love, or romance. Or that we endured the scorn of society just to be inside of you. You want to pretend that your wretched nappy cunt is some grand prize to be had."

"Mine is a prize."

"A prize? We fucked you to relieve ourselves and to make money. You were our breeders, why buy a slave when you can breed your own? When your cunt was on the rag, we fucked your daughters; more than likely they were our daughters, too. Our motive was profit, our pleasure was secondary. Your pleasure was never considered. But we taught you early on how to please us. That's why you're such a good fuck today. That's all you've been trained to do. Pleasure us and make us a profit. That's the real story."

"That's enough, Ian. I don't have to listen to this."

"You are correct. If this makes you uncomfortable, you can walk."

"I'm not walking. There is nothing you can do that would cause me to walk out of here without a contract."

Ian left the room. It was over, Ritz thought.

Ian returned with a pail and a filthy sack dress.

"Take your clothes off," he commanded as he handed Ritz the sack. "Put this on, and then go out in the field and pick some cotton."

"Now you wanna role-play, you sick fuck?!" Ritz yelled. "You know what? We can fuck, but I ain't putting that shit on and I ain't picking shit!"

"If this makes you uncomfortable, don't put on the sack and pick my cotton. And don't get your talk show. Just keep on your labels and leave. Oh, and don't ever come back to Hollywood. The road to your talk show runs right through me. And I'll block you."

Ritz was stuck. How much did she want this really? Now it was a matter of principle. Ritz wasn't leaving until she had her show—and she would get it at any cost. *Play the game.* Ritz was going to play the best Kizzy she knew how. She disrobed on the back porch. She slipped on the scratchy sack dress.

Uh-oh, she was getting hot, and a drop of sweat could reveal all beauty secrets.

That brief walk to Ian's house in the ninety-degree

California heat had bothered Ritz, but she didn't break a sweat; they arrived at Ian's air-conditioned home just in time. However, the midnight cooldown to eighty-six degrees offered no relief from the staggering heat, a hotness that would only be exacerbated by the physical act of picking cotton. She snatched the pail from Ian's hand and marched into the cotton field.

Ritz jump-started her body's sprinkler system just by walking onto the field—the intense heat caused her face and hair to assume minds of their own.

In minutes, Ritz's head-to-toe beauty secrets would be revealed and reversed.

First, sweat trickled down her forehead and onto her eyelids; the fox lashes jumped off her lids and fell to the ground. They resembled little red spiders as a hot and lazy breeze carried them away.

Next, beads of sweat broke through her flawless, shimmery cheeks. Ritz's perfectly blended mineral makeup bonded with the sweat, and the makeup's zinc oxide invaded her pores. Ritz's face stung as if a hundred hands were smacking the hell out of her.

Not that she could scream in pain; Ritz's lips sucked her moisturizing lipstick from the *inside;* and the chapped skin was forming just as quickly on the outside.

From there, Ritz's weave went commando.

Sweat saturated her scalp, causing her roots to revert into tight, coarse miniature coils that gradually separated from the sewn-in weave's tracks. The excessive scalp steam also caused the expensive human-hair weave to revert to *its* natural state, now showing more attributes of My Little Pony doll hair rather than the "virgin cuticle strands from Panama" that Ritz purchased.

Ritz's body sweat caused her sack dress to come alive and irritate her all over, like hungry ants crawling up and down her flesh.

Ritz bent over and examined the strange plants. She pulled down on a burr attached to a plant's stem and twisted the cotton fibers off. She put it in the pail and noticed a dot of crimson—she'd nicked her finger.

Ritz grew tired and weak, and as she bent over to reach for another cotton plant, nausea struck.

She vomited in the field.

Ian stood on the porch and watched Ritz pick cotton. He was enjoying every moment. Even in a sack she was beautiful—elegant even. Her pride wasn't confined to her clothes after all; it was in her walk. It was in her veins. It was even in those tears that streaked her face.

"Connect with your past!" Ian shouted to Ritz. "Humble yourself."

Ian smiled. That ambitious whore would sell her soul for a shot at the tube—they all did. Ian's minidick hardened as he watched his slave-girl fantasy unfurl. He stroked his dick and put on a condom. He stepped out of his khakis and headed into the field, buck-ass naked. Ian fantasized, *I'm gonna fuck that little nigger girl real good in the field.*

He was going to grab her by the hair and drag her back into the house where no one could hear her cry. He would degrade her. Then he'd make that shivering, naked little nigger girl lie across his feet to keep him warm as he slept.

"If it makes you uncomfortable—"

Ritz spun around to see the short, fat, bald, *naked* white man ogling her. Ritz jumped and pounced on Ian, biting, scratching, and mauling him everywhere as he rolled around in the cotton to get away from her.

"I'll make your motherfucking ass uncomfortable!" Ritz yelled. "You like cotton, huh? I'll give you all the cotton you'll ever want."

Ritz smashed Ian's fat back and flat ass with the cotton pail until she knocked him out cold. She enjoyed her handiwork—seeing that fat, naked racist resting atop his beloved bed of cotton plants.

18

Rise

3 A.M.

Ritz couldn't sleep in strange places. She never could. She lay across Ian's bed until she grew tired of hearing him snore out in the field. She rose, carefully peeled the sack dress over her head, and followed the dim light to the parlor; perhaps her clothes were down there. She descended the stairs and, again, came upon the mahogany display case. This time the housekeeper wasn't there to shoo her away.

Ritz opened the door and examined the collectibles. The first item that caught her eye was a postcard. On it was a caricature of a young black girl, braids sticking straight up, and very pregnant. She was in a watermelon patch, with a half-eaten slice in her hand and a devilish grin on her face. The caption read, "I is not expectin'. I's been eatin' melons."

Ritz saw black figurines in sexually suggestive positions. African-caricature Zulu Lulu stirring sticks. A nutcracker fashioned as a buxom black woman; the nut was to be cracked between her legs. And then Ritz found the holy grail of racist paraphernalia, a postcard of a whistling black woman, with bulging eyes and big, ruby lips, and a protruding, pregnant stomach. The caption read, "I went all de way wif L.B.J."

Ritz flipped the card over and it was signed, "Sir Ian, Johnson's darkie Democrats would get a kick out of this revised political slogan!" The author's small print indicated the card surfaced during the 1964 presidential race between Lyndon B. Johnson and Barry Goldwater. Out of her disgust Ritz saw an opportunity. If Ian tried to back out of the deal, she would have proof of what a racist bastard the diversity czar really was.

Ritz swiped the postcard, and still naked as a jaybird, she buried the card deep inside her weave. She latched the cabinet and proceeded to the parlor where she was confronted by the housekeeper.

"You should be in bed, lying across his feet," the mock mammy said.

"I need my clothes," Ritz said coldly. "Role play is over. I want to shower."

"Oh, no, Ritz, I don't want you in my shower."

"You know my name?" Ritz said, surprised.

"We listen to your show all the time. Master Ian loves it. He says that you're good for breaking down black Hollywood on the air all the time. I said, 'How you doin'?' when we first met."

Ritz felt the urge to throw up again but she couldn't. She stood there, naked with a stranger, in a strange house, playing a sick game without knowing the rules.

"What is going on here?" Ritz asked. "You can tell me. I don't understand."

"My opinion is worthless. I dust. I open doors. I lose an occasional bet with Master Ian over someone like you."

"What do you mean?"

"I mean that I never would have expected you to stay here. Master Ian says that black women don't know who they are, that they would do anything to make it. But I told him, not you. I bet him that you would walk because after you were shot your name was splattered all over the airwaves out here. The *Hollywood Reporter* did a full page about your incident, and that perhaps the shooting was just the wake-up call to get you to consider television. Your television show was going to happen with or without Ian; you were a hot commodity all along. But then you strolled right in here and proved him right."

"Um, you won your bet. I whooped Ian's ass. He's sleeping it off in the cotton field. Get my clothes!"

The housekeeper scrambled, "Okay, just don't wake him or I'll be fired."

Ritz might have lost the talk show deal, but she couldn't bear being the ultimate disgrace to everything Maddie had ever tried to teach her. What would Cecil think of her? What would Tracee think? What was Chas thinking now?

Chas! She had to get back to Rutger's. She had to get back to someone she knew.

19

The housekeeper led Ritz to the guest shower. The muted pink and beige decor was just what Ritz needed to calm her insides. She ran the hot shower until the room filled with steam. She found a bar of decorative soap and entered the stall.

To Ritz's surprise, the soap produced invigorating, frothy suds. She caressed her face, neck, and body with the suds, and the stream of hot water massaged her body. The housekeeper entered, delivered Ritz's clothes and some fresh towels, and left.

Every drop of water was bringing Ritz back to life.

After what must have been an eternity for the nervous housekeeper, Ritz shut off the water and exited the stall. She dried off, wiped the steam from the mirror, and was aghast at her appearance. Ashen skin; swollen eyes; dry, cracked lips. Clearly she was dehydrated and had been through a hell of an ordeal.

Ritz stared into the mirror, looking beyond her physical appearance. She rubbed her eyes and gasped at the sight of her mother's reflection.

"Mom?" Ritz whispered. Ritz's mind was spinning. The last time her mother had appeared was when Ritz was in a coma and was this close to joining her mother in the afterlife. So why was she here now?

"Am I dying, Mom?"

Her mother had consoled her last time. But not this time.

"Open your eyes. Know who you are! Don't beg for what is rightfully yours!"

Then her mother was gone.

Ritz gasped. "Open my eyes? Don't beg?"

The housekeeper knocked on the door and Ritz was eager to let her in.

"Come in, please."

"Oh, I thought you'd be dressed," the woman said nervously. "Master Ian is waking up."

"I'm not putting the sack back on. I'm wearing my street clothes, and tell him that I'm not walking to Rutger's."

"You shouldn't have beat him. Master Ian has a long memory."

"Call him master one more time and I'll kick your teeth down your motherfucking throat!" Ritz roared. "Say it again . . . I dare you."

"You can't say that. You've got to stay in character. You won't get your talk show if you talk back to him."

"Whatever."

Ritz reveled in the commotion coming from the cotton field. The naked beast was angry now! Ritz strutted into the den, smashing and wrecking everything in sight. She became the bull in the china shop.

Ian's grunts and heavy steps were growing closer.

"I'm in here, you fat, pasty motherfucker!" Ritz yelled. Her eyes were wild and fierce.

"You bitch! What the fuck are you doing down here?! Annie, call the police! Call the goddamn police!"

Annie was too startled to move. Ritz and her path of destruction had rested at the Wall of Fame. She touched the first picture on the wall.

"Now, wait a goddamn minute, Ritz!" Ian bellowed. "Don't you go messin' with those."

"You like to role-play. You call me by my new name: Sojourner Nat Turner." Ritz tore the end of the picture, threatening to pull it from the wall.

"Ritz . . ."

She ripped it from the wall and placed her hand on the next photo.

"What's my name, bitch?!" she screamed.

"Sojourner!!!"

Ritz ripped the second photo from the wall. "Say my whole name!"

"Sojourner Nat Turner!"

Ritz focused on the stunned housekeeper, who had picked up the phone to dial. "Um, if you dial the cops, I will beat your ass with that phone. I will pulverize your brainless head. In fact, I'll just rip your head off and let your shoulders wear that little mammy hat. Do you understand me? Now get your stupid ass over here and learn something."

The housekeeper moved away from the desk and sat on the couch.

"You ain't allowed to put your black ass on my couch, Annie!" Ian was now fully enraged.

"What you say, motherfucker?" Ritz ripped another picture off the wall and reached for yet another one.

Ian threw up his hands. "I'm sorry. She can sit wherever she wants to."

"Nawl, that's not good enough. Tell her to take her drawers off and rub that nice nappy cunt all over your Italian leather. Go on, tell her!"

Ian hesitated, until Ritz tore another picture.

"Rub your cunt on the couch, Annie."

"If this makes you uncomfortable, you can always leave," Ritz said to her.

The housekeeper removed her pristine, white bloomers.

"That's right," Ritz instructed her. "Rub that cunt all over that couch."

Ian's face was red-hot. "You will never get a show nowhere when I'm done with you," he growled, practically foaming at the mouth. "You won't even get airtime on the public-access channel. You dirty, black, smelly, funky monkey bitch. You fucking nigger monkey whore, dirty rotten, rotten, rotten, filthy, filthy bitch! I will destroy you! You fucking nigger! I will destroy all you fucking nigger bitches. You have no right to live. You are lower than the muddy shit on the bottom of a pig's foot, you rabid slut nasty stupid fucking bitch!"

Ritz watched him with delight. She wanted him to explode.

"Did I tell you that your dick looked like a Q-tip, after I dog-walked your ass in that cotton field?" she squealed.

Ian's veins were playing peekaboo inside his pale forehead. His temples were tap-dancing. He snorted and spat as he came closer to Ritz.

"You fucking breeder. You monkey. You're a petri dish for every disease on this planet!"

Ritz baited him even more. "And yet you can't help but want to fuck each and every one of us."

"You voodoo julu bitch."

"Yeah, we use voodoo to fuck with you." Ritz was enjoying this now. "So what!"

Ian balled his fist. He was well within striking distance now. "If you tear one more autographed photo off my wall, there will be strange fruit hanging in the backyard. Candy-apple red."

Ritz placed one hand on another picture. She stood on her tippy-toes and made her body extralong. She stared at Ian from above. Ritz talked slowly and quietly; she wanted to feed him every word, morsel by morsel.

"You fucked up, Ian. The women on this wall were unknown. They had to take your abuse or go without their big break. But I arrived with the *Ritz Harper Excursion*. I'm not a nobody and I don't need a big break from you. But if you don't play my game, I'll make *you* famous."

The color drained from Ian's face. "You can't threaten me. You'll never work in this industry."

"Mr. Diversity, the only thing that travels faster than gossip is truth. And the truth is, you're the diversity czar with a slave-girl fetish. You have a cotton field in the back of your home. You have sack dresses. You have a throwback mammy to boss around. And you have a shrine with the most vile caricatures that I've ever seen. But do you know what you don't have?"

Ian was silent.

"What you don't have is control. Now, before you fancy bashing my head in and burying me in the cotton field, you should know that everyone in my inner circle knows I'm here. You can't control this situation. You can't control me from tearing every picture off this wall." Ritz ripped another picture. "You can't control the black female image. And most of all, you can't control the fact that I am a queen! And not just any queen, I am the Queen of Radio. I will expose your ass and you will be exiled from Hollywood for the rest of your putrid, worthless life."

In a frenzy, Ritz ripped the remaining pictures off the wall.

"But you can buy my silence. Would you like to deal?"

Ian clenched his jaw. His hands were shaking. He looked terribly weak.

"I asked you, would you like to deal?"

Ian nodded in compliance.

"Good." Ritz walked to Ian's desk. "Where's my contract?"

"Top drawer, to the left," he said feebly.

Ritz found it and began to read. Ian attempted to join the housekeeper on the couch.

"Oh, no, Ian. I want you to stand. Go over and stand on the platform for me."

Ian complied.

Ritz scribbled on some pages and tore the others out. She read aloud as she amended the contract.

"'Ritz Harper is entitled to a traditional pitch meeting with the executive producers of each of the Big Four networks. Ritz Harper is entitled to produce a pilot and six episodes of the show at her home base in New York. Members of her studio audience may include loyal listeners of the *Ritz Harper Excursion*. Ian Hale will pay for all associated production costs. If the first six episodes earn decent ratings, Ritz Harper will be entitled to taping a full season and shopping it to the network of her choice.' "

"That's a fairy tale," Ian said.

Ritz chuckled. "Yeah, but here's a reality check: head of diversity is a racist, chauvinistic pig. Ritz Harper has Ian Hale's two-minute racist rant on her hidden camera phone.

"You know, Ian, what I say over the air is like a burp in the breeze. But once this shit hits the Internet, it lives on forever." Ritz glowered at Ian. "Deal, or no deal? If any of this makes you feel uncomfortable, I could walk."

"Give me the fucking papers!"

"Oh, and you may want to dig up that cotton field, to show what a good sport you are. I'd like to see those racist relics destroyed, too—all of them. I don't give a damn about your little throwback mammy. If she wants to hang around and feed your slave fetish, that's on her. I don't stand up for dumb-asses."

"I'm not dumb," Annie objected. "Ian, you've gotta give me a little somethin' to keep quiet, too."

Ian spun around to look at Annie. "And what in the fuck do you want?"

She grinned like a Cheshire cat as she squirmed in her seat. "I want this couch."

20

Jungle

Chas and Rutger fell asleep on the floor of the study. If it was cold, the men didn't know it. Their intimate spoon position provided all the body heat that they needed. Rutger's shrieking cell phone pierced the silence.

Chas's phone was going off, too.

"Hello?" Rutger answered. There was a long pause. "She did what?!"

Chas didn't answer his phone. He already knew it was about Ritz, and he already knew it was bad. Rutger ended the call and pulled away from Chas's warm, naked ass.

"Get up. Put on your clothes. Ian's driver is bringing Ritz."

"What happened?" Chas really wanted to know.

Rutger didn't look at Chas as he located his clothes. "It's not what happened that concerns me. It's what happens next."

Chas checked his cell phone. It wasn't Ritz who was calling him after all. It was Ruff. And his message was ominous: "Chas, it's Ruff. Look, um, Michelle Davis may be filling in for Ritz for the entire week. No rotations. We like her."

Fuck! Chas dialed Ritz's cell. She picked up on the first ring.

"Where you at?" he asked.

"We're pulling up in front of Rutger's place now. Get your shit, Chas. We need to get out of here."

Ian instructed his driver, Bill, to take Chas and Ritz back to the L'Ermitage in Beverly Hills. The two sat silently, not uttering a word, until they were back at their hotel.

21

SATURDAY, 7:50 A.M.

BEVERLY HILLS, CALIFORNIA

L'ERMITAGE HOTEL

RITZ'S GOVERNOR SUITE

Ritz and Chas remained silent in the lobby. They rode the elevator, which had a few other guests, without a word. But one step inside Ritz's suite and they exploded with the excitement of two schoolgirls, peppering their talk with an assortment of expletives.

Ritz wanted to go first.

"Chas, I did it!" Ritz shouted. "I've got the pitch meeting lined up for Monday."

"You were with him just to get a pitch meeting? Ritz, what went down over there? I know he called Rutger."

Ritz told Chas everything—except picking cotton, and kicking the guy's ass—but she told him everything else.

"And so he presents this generic contract that promises a meeting with network staff members and then he's released of his obligations," Ritz continued. "I told him, fuck that. I arrived on his doorstep with fame and a following, and I wanted a real opportunity. I negotiated into the contract that I would get the pilot, a glowing recommendation from his New Actor's Guild, and a set pitch meeting with executive producers from the Big Four networks on Monday. And I told him that if he didn't meet my terms, then I would tell my radio audience about his little slave-girl fetish."

"What slave-girl fetish?"

Oops. Ritz was silent, then said, "Chas, I'm getting a shot at my talk show. I fucking did it!"

"Ritz, you can't bully your way into a hit talk show. These people are going to play your game, but believe me, they will do everything to make sure you fail. Ritz, you won't win!"

"Why did you bring me here if you didn't think I would win?"

"You were challenging my clout, Ritz. I brought you here just to show you I had some. I wanted you to meet Rutger—and, fuck it, that was a good excuse for me to see him again, too."

"You brought me here just to front, Chas? Just to front?"

"If you wanna put it that way, fine. I know you can't handle Hollywood. Rutger told me that. No one likes you, you don't have a presence, and it's not a good idea to take a chance on this shit with Michelle Davis sitting in your chair all week back at WHOT."

The earth moved under her toes. Ritz knew instantly that Michelle Davis wasn't just filling in, she was auditioning for the throne.

"What did you say?"

"Ruff called," Chas said. "Abigail wants Michelle to fill in for you—all week. She's sick of running the 'Best Of' shows. Gossip has to be done every day, man. You can't keep running that old Whitney Houston interview."

"You've got to fix it, Chas; you've got to make it work. I can't go back to scrapping for airtime with some half-rate newshound bitch that they're going to replace me with anyway. Don't you see what's happening here? Behind Door A is a new possibility. Behind Door B is a new possibility. Both possibilities are unknown."

"You're losing me, Ritz."

"Okay, it's a possibility that I may strike a talk show deal out here in California. There's a possibility that I may return to WHOT and get demoted or worse because of the drama that's been happening outside of the studio."

On that note, Chas lowered his head and massaged his temples. "We need to order some breakfast. All I taste is Rutger."

"Eeew. You're nasty, Chas!"

Ritz called room service.

Before and during their breakfast of French toast, orange juice, and scrambled eggs, the two went back and forth over the pros and cons of delving into something new versus returning to something successful.

Finally, Ritz got to the bottom of their disagreement. "I get it now. It's us in New York. It's me out here. Chas, I don't know the first thing about television shows, or producing one, but after spending one night in this town, I know that I need a familiar face around me. Don't you get it? It would be us here *and* back at home."

Chas wasn't falling for it, not this time, not ever again after Ritz stayed behind at Ian's place. Ian was right: They were two people in the same place at the same time, but they were not together. They were not a team.

"Here's the deal, Ritz. It's Saturday. I'm packing my bags tonight and I will be at WHOT tomorrow. If you're not there, I will start making moves to produce Michelle Davis. I'll prep her for your slot. Trust."

Ritz stood over Chase as he ate. "Are you threatening me, motherfucker? I'm the star, Chas. *I'm* the star!"

"That's right. You're the star and you're going to do what you want to do no matter who you hurt or who you leave behind. But I'm the star *maker*, Ritz. I'm going to get mine, going forward. I'm not pouring no more of my energy into you. That's it."

"I can't be at two doors at once, Chas."

"Yeah, one door is closing and the other one will never open. Now pick one."

Chas exited her suite without completing his breakfast, saying good-bye, or taking the food cart to the hall. Funny, when they traveled for the award shows, Chas always took the food cart out of Ritz's room. He knew how funny she was about dirty plates. But now he just didn't give a damn.

Ritz rolled the food cart into the hall, and before she knew it, the door slammed behind her. She was locked out of her suite. She went to the front desk to get another key. The clerk also handed Ritz a certified letter from Ian Hale. She returned to the suite and opened her letter; it was a confirmed itinerary for her pitch session with the Big Four executive producers, on Monday at 11 a.m., at the Big Four headquarters.

She was excited, scared, confused. She knew she would have to go it alone this time. Ritz called the only person who ever had her back no matter what. Tracee.

22

SATURDAY, 8:53 A.M.
BEVERLY HILLS, CALIFORNIA
L'ERMITAGE HOTEL
CHAS'S SUITE

Chas lay on the bed fully clothed, reeking of sex and cologne. Partying with Rutger didn't feel the way it had before. And he knew better than to try to hook up again after Hurricane Ritz had fucked up with Ian. So he lay there. Struggling to digest his breakfast. Struggling to make sense of it all—his life, his lays, his longing for something more stable than the *Excursion*.

The writing was on the wall: Ritz was going to roll with television. He was going to be ass out. So now what?

As Chas dosed off, his phone vibrated and woke him. It was a text from Hardcore: "I'm in the lobby."

Chas texted his suite number, then bolted out of bed. Before he could hop in the shower and freshen up, there was a knock at the door. Chas's stomach fell to his feet. He knew it was Hardcore. And he knew he wasn't ready for any new company.

Hardcore knocked again. "Hey, Chas, it's me dude."

Chas slowly opened the door. "Hey . . ."

"Oh, it's like that?" Hardcore teased, pointing to Chas's disheveled appearance. "You wanna wash up first, nigga?"

Rutger had fucked Chas to sleep. But now all he could think about was climbing Hardcore. The thought alone was a zap of caffeine delivered right to his dick.

"Make yourself at home," Chas said, heading to the shower. "I'll just be a minute."

The studio-gangsta-turned-novice-assassin unlocked the safety from the Russian Baikal converted 9 mm handgun. He screwed on the silencer. He hid the gun inside the invisible inside ankle pocket of his cargo pants.

As the shower ran, Hardcore crept about the room looking for Ritz's room number, or better yet a spare key. Hardcore was fumbling through the papers on the end table when the shower abruptly stopped. Chas, refreshed and sopping wet, smiled as he did his peacock stroll to the bed. Hardcore was already there, fully dressed.

"Take that towel off," Hardcore demanded.

Oh, here we go again, Chas thought to himself. Chas was a little on the feminine side, with a slight build and an elegant demeanor, but he was no bottom. When the lights went down, he was in control (except when he was with Rutger, and he still couldn't explain that). The one-night stands often mistook him for the receiver. But Chas would let them know quickly what he was about.

"You take *your* pants off," Chas said, not budging an inch to remove his towel.

Hardcore didn't move. "Come here, lil' nigga, and take them off me."

That sent shivers down Chas's spine. And he was not too eager to fuck and was too tired to fight. He dropped the towel and crawled over to him. Hardcore surprised himself with how turned on he was. And it made him uncomfortable.

His chocolate brown dick was bulging in his pants. He spread he knees farther apart to situate himself. He didn't want that faggot Chas to touch him, but then again, his dick wanted him right now.

Chas's slender fingers toyed with Hardcore's zipper. In a stealth motion, Hardcore lifted his behind so that the cargo pants would fall midcalf. Hardcore heard the soft clink of the gun when his ankle tapped the leg of the chair.

Chas didn't hear anything at all. He wasn't paying attention to anything except the heavy rhythmic breathing from Hardcore's lips. Why tease? Chas dove right in with random sucking motions. Hardcore was growing weak, his eyes turned to stone and his neck turned to jelly. He wanted some ass. Enough of the mouth shit.

Hardcore stood back. "Bend over."

Chas refused. He was too sore from Rutger and he wanted some ass, too. "You bend over."

"What kind of game you playin', bitch? Turn the fuck around and let me take care of this," Hardcore demanded, one hand on his throbbing dick.

"No, baby. I'm not taking it. I've giving it!"

Hardcore raged, "You wanna give me what, faggot?!"

He punched Chas square in his nose. Chas was in a daze. Hardcore picked him up and threw him on the bed, sending the replica Lotus lamp crashing to the floor.

"Open that ass, nigga! I don't know who in the fuck you think you playing with!"

Chas's bloody nose stained the pillow.

Hardcore stepped out of one leg of his jeans. He spat into Chas's ass crack and climbed on top of the small man, punching him in the back of the head and neck to control him. He shoved his dick into Chas's ass, not caring that it was hurting him, too.

Chas screamed, only to get punched again.

Caught up in the rapture of his own rage, Hardcore didn't hear the faint click of the hotel door. In an instant, a flood of light filled the room. Weapons drawn, LAPD officers demanded the thug rapper "Freeze" before he got his head blown off.

Chas was in a heap on the bed, bloody, bruised, and battered from head to toe.

"We'll get you an ambulance, sir," said a black cop who had his gun still trained on Hardcore. "Don't move, Hardcore! Put your hands in the air!"

Oh shit, they know who I am! Hardcore's dick went soft. He held his hands up in the air. "May I pull up my pants?"

"Do it slowly," the cop responded.

Hardcore knew now that there was no denying the gay rumors. But worse than that, he would now be known as a rapist, too. He put his leg back inside his pants and pulled them up. He felt the gun inside the inner ankle pocket, and in one swift motion he pulled it out and stuck it under his chin.

"Put the gun down!" the officers yelled. A barrage of threats followed.

"Fuck y'all," Hardcore yelled as he pulled the trigger.

23

Ritz Harper's ego couldn't stand the turbulence. She'd had to put her foot down with a British swinger, a racist diversity czar with a slave-girl fetish, and now Chas. Chas broke her heart. She couldn't believe that he—the man who'd helped her get here, the man who was behind her career from the beginning—would bring her to L.A. just to prove that she wasn't good enough for television. Chas wanted those animals to break her down because he couldn't do it alone. And then he threatened to return to the studio to produce Michelle Davis, her replacement?

If the Queen of Radio couldn't trust her producer, whom could she trust?

The spa masseur came highly recommended. Perhaps he could be her confidant for sixty minutes and help her not only work out the kinks in her sore muscles (that ass-whupping of Ian had taken something out of Ritz, too), but could also help her work out the kinks in her career. Ritz laughed to herself.

A gorgeous Jamaican spa attendant approached Ritz. She looked desperate.

"Ms. Harper?!"

"Yes, baby," Ritz said, furrowing her brow. "What's wrong?"

"You have a visitor. Please come to the office."

"A visitor? I'm at the spa," Ritz protested. "Can they come back later? I really need this massage."

"I'm sorry, ma'am, this isn't a social call."

Ritz secured her plush robe around her frame and followed the young woman into the spa's management office. A butch cop awaited her. The officer was as tall as Ritz, but wide. She had a short haircut, a tight jacket, and a grim look on her face.

"Ms. Harper, I'm homicide detective Maddow—"

"Homicide! What? Who? Where's Chas?!"

"Have a seat, ma'am."

Ritz couldn't move. The officer placed a firm hand on Ritz's shoulder and forced her to sit.

"Ms. Harper, we are investigating the suicide of Christopher Hardcore Harris—"

"What?! Oh my God! Is it my fault?"

"NYPD homicide detective Pelov arranged for LAPD officers to monitor you while you were at this hotel. His concern was that your traveling partner, Mr. Chas James, and your stalker, Mr. Harris, might do you harm. Our officers noticed Christopher Hardcore Harris arrive at the hotel, and we put someone outside your door. We observed Harris enter Mr. James's suite—"

"He broke into Chas's suite?"

"No, ma'am. Mr. James invited him inside. A sexual assault took place, and when confronted by our officers, Mr. Harris produced a weapon and committed suicide."

"Stop." Ritz was having a hard time catching her breath. "Chas was with the man that threatened to kill me?"

"Ma'am, hotel staff verified that the two had dinner on the terrace the night before."

Tears of anger and betrayal rushed down Ritz's face. The officer left and returned with a small spa towel. She handed it to Ritz.

"Ms. Harper, Detective Pelov wants to debrief you when you return to New York. Here's my card. We are confident that the immediate danger is over. However, our mayor sends the message that he is a fan of yours, and that L.A.'s finest will be watching over you while you're here. It will be from afar, ma'am. We know you may want to keep a low profile."

Ritz swallowed hard. "Where is he now?"

"Chas James is at the Beverly Hills short-term hospital. We can arrange for someone to take you there—"

"No, thank you. He fucked with a snake, and he became one. If I never see Chas James again in my lifetime, it would be too soon."

The officer sat beside her. "You know, ma'am, I see ugliness all the time. I see the worst of what people can do to one another. And I know that all of this is hard. But there is another day ahead of you. And soon it will be Monday, the best day of the week!"

Ritz shook her head. "Monday is the best day? Well, okay."

"Yeah, I always tell my colleagues to celebrate Mondays because there are so many people who don't make it past the weekend," Detective Maddow said. "Monday is the first day of the best of your life."

24

It's Getting WHOT in Here

MONDAY, 8:59 A.M.
NEW YORK CITY
WHOT STUDIOS

Michelle Davis adjusted her headset and cleared her throat, took a sip of water and prepared to sign off. She was filling in this day on Veronica Villagomez's *V Spot* morning-drive show. She was going to do a double shift today as she kicked off the week in the Queen's chair—filling in for Ritz Harper.

"This is Michelle Davis, and I thank you for allowing us to take you away on the *V Spot*. Remember, if you miss a minute, you miss a lot." The outro music, Beyoncé's "Irreplaceable," sent her off the air.

"Wait, Michelle, we have some breaking news!"

Tony, the engineer, said, commanding the mic (and turning Michelle's mic off).

"Everybody, this is Ritz Harper, of the *Ritz Harper Excursion,* and we have breaking news!" The Los Angeles Police Department had managed to keep the rape and suicide out of the press long enough for Ritz to have the scoop. It wasn't done purposely. They couldn't release the information until Hardcore's next of kin were notified. But it worked out perfectly for Ritz, who couldn't wait to pounce.

"Rapper Hardcore was just busted for the attempted rape of our producer, Chas James, in his Beverly Hills suite! Chas is in the ICU, but Hardcore blew his head off. Again, Hardcore committed suicide after being caught in the act by the LAPD, raping our producer, Chas James!"

Tony flicked Michelle's mic on. Michelle was stunned. "Ritz, is Chas hurt?"

"Chas will pull through just fine, honey," Ritz said. "His phatty buddies know that Chas is a topper, so his, um, ass will be in pain for a while."

Ruff rushed into the studio and said, *"Hang up on that tacky bitch, now, or you're all fired!"* It was live and over the air.

"What did he say—," Ritz managed, before Tony dropped her call.

Nanoseconds later the in-house phone rang. It was the Three Suits notifying Ruff that there would be a companywide meeting on Tuesday.

25

The Gift

MONDAY, 10:45 A.M.
LOS ANGELES
BEVERLY HILLS MEDICAL CENTER

Chas had gone from being almost famous to instantly famous in a few hours. His rape and Hardcore's suicide was on every television station and on the radio. Chas had to admit, the thug rapper/rapist was too juicy of a story to pass up. Ritz fed the wire every morsel of the crime. She was right smack in the middle of it all.

But she hadn't called him. The nurses were angry on Chas's behalf. One male nurse, Conner, treated Chas well and tried his best not to humiliate him during the rape-kit process.

Several hours later, Conner returned and coun-
seled, "You have every right to sue her, for breach of
privacy. Rape victims have privacy laws in California.
Don't worry, attorney Gloria Allred is going to get in
her ass!"

Just the word *ass* made Chas cringe. "That's the
fabulous Queen of Radio," Chas lamented. "Ratings
and raises. That's all she cares about."

Conner took the remote out of Chas's hand. "That
knot on your forehead is coming down nicely. And I
bet your face looks better than the other guy's."

Chas would smile at the attempted comic relief but
he was in too much pain. The doctor, a top-heavy
Middle Eastern woman with a long, neat braid and
sporty glasses, entered the room and washed her
hands. She spoke with a thick accent.

"Okaaayyy. Mr. James, I am Dr. Patel, a resident
here. And I want to go over the results of your rape kit
with you."

"I don't want to hear it. I know, I've been torn here
and stretched there. I can feel it."

She examined his eyes with her miniflashlight. She
felt his lymph nodes. Chas jerked in pain. He could
still feel Hardcore's fist crash-landing on the back of
his head.

"I'm sorry, just checking." Dr. Patel scribbled in the
chart. "We'll get some more Percodan in your drip,
you'll feel better, okay? Now, Mr. James, what protease
inhibitors are you taking?"

"What?"

"Are you on any kind of combo routine?"

"No. I get high occasionally, and I drink."

"Are you not taking drug therapy of any kind?"

Chas was insulted. What happened to the post-race society? "No. We're not all crackheads!" he said sternly to the doctor.

Dr. Patel placed the chart on the bed and sighed. "Oh, my goodness, you don't know, do you? Mr. James, you are HIV-positive."

"H-I-V?!" Chas repeated aloud.

The doctor might as well have said D-I-E.

Chas's mind zipped to the sexcapades—there had been so many of them lately—when passion took control of his better judgment. The intoxicating mix of greed and dick lust, pursuit and conquest, had led to this—a hospital bed that might as well have been placed inside a hospice.

"I fucked up," Chas said to himself, then to the doctor.

"I fucked up," Chas said to the God that he didn't pray to so often. "Damn!"

Dr. Patel listened patiently as Chas went through the motions. Her bedside manner wasn't what it should have been. The detachment was the last thing Chas needed. He needed comfort. He needed someone to put a hand on his shoulder and tell him it was going to be all right. But she sat there with a blank stare on her face as he went through about five different emotions: shock, anger, sadness, confusion, and finally despair.

Dr. Patel did have one strength—the ability to connect with the eccentric. That skill served her well in Beverly Hills.

"You don't have to die, Mr. James. This is an ailment, a condition that can be controlled to some extent. There are many people living long, healthy lives with HIV."

"I've seen too many people go. The gift can't be trusted. One person is gone in a matter of weeks, while somebody else can hang on, still kicking it like Magic Johnson. How do I know which gift I've got? How do I know how long I've had it?"

Dr. Patel tried to bond with him. "Why do you call it a gift, Chas?"

"Some gay men think that AIDS is gonna kill 'em anyway, so they want to fuck around with somebody who already has it. The gift grants sexual freedom."

Dr. Patel was visibly disturbed. "Freedom? How so?"

"If you know you're positive, you don't fear getting it anymore. No more precautions; you can just do your thang. But I didn't ask for the gift."

Chas turned his head away from Dr. Patel. A tear raced out of the corner of his eye and disappeared into the pillow.

"How do I tell the men I've been with . . . 'Oh, I'm sorry, I may have given the gift to you.' Or, how do I face who could have given it to me?"

"Mr. James, we can help contact whoever you need to contact. Do you have any idea who could have exposed you to the virus?"

"How the fuck do I know?!" he yelled, striking the bed with his fists, embarrassed that he had been so careless over the years that it could literally be one of a dozen men. "What the fuck! I don't hurt anybody. And look at what happened to me. *Who would do this to me?!*"

Chas's rant echoed through the halls. Dr. Patel was silent, not knowing what to say, not wanting to trigger any more outbursts.

"You know, I knew I'd go out young," he said. "But not like this. This shit is humiliating. I'm embarrassed. I can't go to the clubs, or hook up, none of that. I will be an outcast."

Outcast was the buzzword that Dr. Patel was waiting for—she heard it often among her Beverly Hills patients and knew how to manipulate the sentiment to her advantage.

"Oh no, Mr. James. You're not an outcast. You can be in the forefront. Magic Johnson is a spokesman. You can go around and speak to people, too. You're a young man, a handsome man with many friends. I suppose that you can take this gift—as you call it—and turn it into something positive. You can make a difference. There are organizations that I know that are in dire need of a voice to speak to the many . . . you would be perfect."

"Shiiiiittttt!" Chas was beyond angry, and dismissive.

"Someone hooked me up and now I'm supposed to put my name out there as the AIDS poster child? I'm supposed to give up my life to look out for everybody else? I don't think so!" The undercurrent of evil was surfacing. "Whoever did this to me didn't look out for me. Didn't give me a heads-up. Nobody told me shit!"

Dr. Patel scribbled in Chas's file, then shoved it under her arm. She left his side to wash her hands— and to get away from him. His venomous attitude was seeping out from every pore of his body like a funky mist, threatening to envelop anything in its path.

"I have one thing to say, Mr. James," Dr. Patel said. "The best option, always, is to take care of yourself and live a meaningful life. Bitterness worsens the suffering."

"Nobody told me shit," said Chas, now almost in a trance of his own anger. "So I ain't gonna tell nobody shit, either."

Dr. Patel's eyes grew wide. "I must inform you that intentionally infecting someone with HIV is a crime in the state of California, Mr. James. You will go to jail."

"I know," Chas said with a menacing grin. "But I live and fuck in New York!"

26

Fame

Ritz Harper and her best friend, Tracee Remington, were polar opposites. Tracee had that chameleon sex appeal, like Janet Jackson. One minute Tracee was grown and sexy à la Janet in her famous "Pleasure Principle" video; but the next minute she was the ponytail-wearing, dimpled-cutie-pie Janet, à la Penny from *Good Times*. Either way, the brown-skinned natural beauty with the thousand-watt smile, almond eyes, and thick, curly hair always had a halo.

The two friends also had opposing career ambitions. Ritz wanted to conquer more of the entertainment world, whereas Tracee, the youngest, most successful black music rep at Uni-Global, accepted a lucrative early-retirement package and moved to Winter Garden, Florida, to find herself.

Little did Ritz know, Tracee had also been finding herself in the throes of a long-distance relationship with Randolph Jordan, Ritz's half brother. Tracee and Randolph were spending the weekends together at his place in Jersey.

Tracee was en route to the grocery store when Ritz called her cell.

"Oh my goodness! Is Chas all right?" Tracee said. "It's all over the news out here. *You're* all over the news! I don't agree with you telling the world he was raped."

"The story isn't what you think it is," Ritz said.

"I am disgusted by this. And you know I usually stay out of your way when you gossip. But, no, no, no! I would not be your friend if I didn't tell you that you crossed the line this time. This isn't entertainment, Ritz, this is a man's life—a man who is close to you."

"Tray, there's a lot going on—"

"Let me tell you what's going on right now. Michelle Davis is on your show, the *Ritz Harper Excursion*, and she's asking *your* listeners if you were foul and out of line by disrespecting Chas. *Your* audience is siding with her. Chas is the victim here and you crossed the line."

"You think I did this for no reason? Tray, you know me better than that."

"I don't know what I know about you when ratings are involved."

Silence.

"I know your next move," Tracee said. "You're going to hang up the phone and cut me off because I don't agree with you. Ritzy, anyone who agrees with you a hundred percent of the time is not looking out for your best interest. They are sponges. I love you. I care about you, and even if you hate me, I will be that one person who won't leave you. Now, hang up on me if you want to. I'll still answer the phone when you're mature enough to call me back."

Silence.

"I can hear you breathing," Tracee said. "And I'm not hanging up."

Ritz was fighting between anger and pain. She wanted Tracee to understand. She *needed* Tracee to understand.

"When I was shot, Chas wrote the press release and gave interviews," Ritz finally broke the silence. "When I discovered I was pregnant, Chas developed a promotion around 'Who's Her Baby's Daddy?' When I lost my baby, Chas wrote the press release and suggested that I make appearances and start a foundation for stars who lost their children. It was never about what was best for me! He just used my life events to generate buzz."

"He was your producer. He wasn't obligated to be your friend. This is the industry you're in."

"I know this. I expected him to use my life events to promote himself. But when he mixed it up with Hardcore, he was orchestrating my biggest life event ever—my death."

Tracee sighed and took a deep breath. "I'm not surprised."

"Why aren't you surprised?" Ritz *was* surprised by Tracee's response.

"I can't put my finger on it, Ritz. It's something that I saw back when you were in the coma. I was with your Auntie M., Cecil, and Chas. We were trying to see you when that homicide detective approached us. There was a moment when he explained that he was assigned to the case because originally you flatlined. . . ."

"Go on."

"I don't want to assail his character, but we all expressed relief when we found out that you came back. And Chas didn't seem relieved at all. It was as if he was in shock that you made it. And then he got on his cell phone and walked into the hallway. He was yelling the entire time. Finally the nurse told him to get off the phone because he was in a hospital."

There was silence.

"So I told that detective that Chas's response made me leery. I felt bad about reporting that, but I had to. Ritzy, are you there? Ritzy?"

"I-I-I just can't understand it. Why didn't you tell me?!"

"I wasn't sure. It was just a feeling. And he seemed

to be doing right by you and your career. I told myself I would watch him, and if I saw anything else out of the ordinary, I would confront him myself."

"He brought me all the way out here to tear me down." Ritz was now retracing everything, going over every movement and detail of Chas's actions in her head. "But if he didn't want me alive, well, then it all makes sense."

"You say Chas brought you there? Well, Michelle Davis has been saying on the radio that you forced Chas to come with you to L.A. Ruff mentioned on the air that it was you that requested the time off and refused to let Chas stay behind to work with Michelle."

"Nobody believes that bullshit, do they?"

"Everybody believes it. It looks pretty bad, Ritz. Michelle said Hardcore was stalking you. He kidnapped and tortured Chas, but Chas wouldn't tell him where you were. Chas was looking out for you, but you turned around and gossiped about his ordeal. She has you looking pretty bad."

"Ruff gave an interview to Michelle?"

"Yes, he did. And he said that Chas's friends are circulating petitions to change the name of your show from the *Ritz Harper Excursion* to just the *Excursion*."

"Tray, I promise you, that is not what happened at all." Ritz was in disbelief. "I am the victim here. They are using my show, and my audience, to launch a hate campaign against me. I don't know how to fight back because they're all against me."

* * *

For the first time in a long time, Ritz Harper had a real conversation with her best friend; and she told Tracee the truth about everything.

"I never thought Chas would go there. But, why not? Street producers who are looking to move some units will stage a crime or plant some drugs on their low-level talent. When that talent's arrest is splashed across the media, the label gets a buzz. Imagine how a producer's stock would rise if his star talent was gunned down right in the midst of a ratings war!"

"Ritz, this treachery takes me back to the shadiness that I had to deal with at Uni-Global. And you know what saved me? I built a Go-Getter garden: Dig up those weeds of self-doubt. Cultivate the soil of spirituality. Plant that seed of faith. And nurture your garden daily with hard work and good deeds. Do that for yourself, Ritz, if you want to be successful."

Ritz didn't have a clue about what Tracee was saying. It sounded so hokey. But she managed to respond, "I will."

"Don't worry." Tracee knew her friend better than she knew herself. "I will help you every step of the way. I will show you what to do. It doesn't happen overnight. It takes time. You're on your way home now, right?"

"Not right away. I have a pitch meeting today with the Big Four. I'm going to do that, and then I'm heading back to fight for my job, if I still have one."

"I don't think it's a good idea to go to the pitch meeting."

"Why? Because you don't think I'm good for television, either?"

"No, actually, I think you're absolutely perfect for television. I see that for you. My concern is all that's taken place since you've been there. And I don't like how you came into the contract. I have a lot of contacts in television. Remember, you're on my old stomping ground. My advice is for you to just drop the meeting and come back home. Those studio folks will waste your time. You have some work to do back here first."

Ritz was dumbstruck. Of course, Tray knew everything about everybody in Los Angeles. If it was television that Ritz wanted, she should have started with Tray. But now too much dirt was going on behind the scenes and Ritz wanted to keep Tray out of it.

"Are you there, Ritzy? Did you hear me? Get out of L.A., now."

"What? And come this far for nothing? Have all of that drama go down and I come back with nothing to show for it? I'm going to the pitch meeting tomorrow, and then I'll come back."

"Fuck that!" Tracee yelled, shocking Ritz. "If someone put a hit on you before, they can have someone finish the job out there. Get the fuck out of L.A. right now. Throw your shit in a bag and leave that hotel. When you get to LAX, reschedule your pitch meeting with the Big Four, and I promise that I'll go with you."

"Okay, okay, Tray. Why are you cussin'? You're scaring me."

"And, Ritz, do *not* talk to anyone from WHOT. Don't worry about that chick warming up your throne. *I've got this!*"

27

The Pitch

Monday, the first day of the best of her life. That's what that detective said, right? Ritz Harper only knew how to act and react, which was a strong suit in the rough-and-tumble world of shock radio. But shock jockism doesn't translate well in a pitch meeting. One false move, one misunderstood comment, one flat joke, one cuss word, one Ritz-ism, and she could be out on her ass.

Ritz knew this, which is why she never pitched herself—and would never go by herself. She was overly critical, and so accustomed to tripping people up when she asked them questions, that she always feared someone would turn the tables on her. In her mind, some people were just out to get her.

One such band of Ritz-haters were the Jennifers.

The Jennifers, as Ritz called them, were the cadre of usually young, thin, sometimes white music-label execs who always served as the gatekeepers to the big-wigs and artists, even though they didn't know shit about shit. And the ones that really worked her nerves were often named Jennifer, or Jan, or Jo, or the occasional Jose.

Early in Ritz's career, she had to battle with them all the time. The Jennifers may have been dumb, but as a rule they were bold. If they didn't like an interview or how their client was portrayed, the Jennifers would work the phones, launching complaints to management and blocking Ritz from accessing their other major stars. Now that Ritz had the number one show, the Jennifers were powerless—the tables were turned and the Jennifers needed to get their artists on the *Excursion,* no matter what the outcome.

It stood to reason that the Jennifers existed in network television as well, and Ritz worried about her inability to hold her temper. When Ritz got frustrated, she lost control—cuss words, low-down digs, yo' mama jokes, anything and everything would simmer in her mind, then explode from her lips. Chas could see the tsunami of rage before it overflowed, and he was always there to catch her and stop her. Chas wasn't here for her now.

Her beloved Auntie M. taught her to hold her tongue, to lock it behind her teeth before she said something ugly. Auntie M. wasn't here either. And unfortunately, that strategy hadn't really worked for Ritz thus far. Ritz had a dilemma.

Should she follow Tracee's advice and pack it up and come home and wage this war another time? Or would she get what she came for and not leave until she had it?

She was going to stay and take her spotlight back. Now her dilemma was how. How was she going to do it? Which Ritz should she display? Should she be the confident Queen of Radio, boisterous, loud, funny, and shocking? What if the execs misunderstood her New York brash and flavor?

Or would Ritz be Ritgina, the laid-back lady Auntie M. inspired? Could she emulate Tracee and be real, down-to-earth, and allow her fabulousness to reveal itself sporadically? Or would Ritz turn up the heat without turning them off?

It was too bad that the old, loyal Chas wasn't around. Chas always seemed to guide Ritz, such as instructing her not to wear the "best of her star shit" when doing charity functions, or how to properly display her fabulous tits when she was working the red carpet.

And with Tracee's experience with prepping her roster of misfit music celebrities, she would be a huge help right about now as well. But this new fire-and-brimstone Tracee seemed out of touch with the real world. Ritz couldn't call her to get her advice on this after Tracee was adamant about Ritz's not going. And she was adamant. Ritz had never heard the Bible-thumper cuss like that before—even *before* she found the Lord!

"So what's a diva to do?" Ritz said aloud to herself. She scanned her wardrobe that she'd hung neatly in the large walk-in closet of her suite.

"If I dress too fabulously, the Jennifers may hate me. If my clothes are boring, the Jennifers may fall asleep. Hmm . . .

"Red says I know I've got it going on, or that I'm a bitch. Pink says that I'm a team player but meek. Black says I'm playing it safe and trying to look thin."

Finally, an ensemble spoke to her.

The chocolate Prada pantsuit. Elegant and comfortable; the slim seams and the straight legs worked well with Ritz's long frame. She was powerful, without looking masculine. And the cut slimmed her hips and waist. Ritz paired the suit with a cream Chanel bow blouse, a birthday gift from Chas—how fitting.

Tiny pearl earrings and simple chocolate heels completed her look.

Ritz longed for something hot pink to wear. Pink was her power color, it made her feel ultrafeminine and ferocious. Those good feelings would come while she was being roasted by the Jennifers, that's for sure. Ritz donned her bright pink and leopard La Perla Malizia bra and panty set.

Ritz looked at herself in the full-length mirror. She was pleased with what she saw.

"Now it's time to beat this face, girl!" she said to herself. Putting on her makeup was always a challenge for Ritz. One of the benefits of being the Queen of Radio was that she didn't have to wear makeup every day. Only when the cute guys came by—the cute straight guys—did Ritz really try to accentuate her positives. When she was on the red carpet, a makeup artist handled everything.

On her own, Ritz had never quite mastered the art, and it was an art. She tried to remember what her makeup artist had told her about the nighttime vamp look versus the daytime natural look. Usually, when Ritz applied her own makeup, she opted for the night-time look—fox-fur eyelashes, painted rouge cheeks, heavy Prince black eyeliner, day or night.

Not today, however. Ritz was not going to go over-board. "Just a dab will do ya, all around," she told herself.

Ritz examined her face, her eyes, her forehead. The swelling was long gone, and that was good; the wrinkles hadn't formed and that was really good. Concealer, pat, pat pat . . . powder, and nude gloss. Clean up the brows with her tweezers, fill in the thin areas, (just as Chas had taught her), and add a little gold dust, just a little.

Okay, just a little more gold dust.

Ritz took the glitter brush and dabbed her cheeks,

her chin, her forehead. The glitter looked so hot, she thought. She sparkled like a goddess.

Ritz studied her reflection and made random faces. (A bad habit of radio deejays was saying one thing while their expression said another. In the studio, as long as the voice came through, no one gave a damn about the faces they were making, but that could be hazardous at a pitch meeting!) Ritz smiled. "Pleased to meet you," she practiced. Now she was serious. *Okay, throw your head back and to the left when laughing.* Ritz was confident that smile wasn't fake and that her "serious look" wasn't too forced. The self-critique continued.

"Hi, I'm Ritz Harper," she said to the mirror. *No, too confident. You can't walk in the door like you have the damn show in syndication already!*

"Hi, I'm Ritgina Harper," she said to the mirror. *What the fuck is a Ritgina? Good Lord. Black mothers sure know how to fuck up their children's names.*

"Okay, let's try the Tracee route," she said to herself. "I'm Ritzy!"

Ritz clapped her hands like a high school cheerleader. "Gimme a R . . . I . . . T . . . Z . . . Y.

"Gimme a Y . . ."

Gimme a Y? "Are you tripping, you silly bitch?" Ritz laughed to herself. She welcomed the laughter and the silliness. It definitely broke her anxiety.

"Fuck it," she said. "We'll just go with the flow."

The hotel phone rang, signaling that her car had arrived.

"Okay, we're on!" Ritz gave herself one last once-over. "Let's go get what we came for."

Ritz walked out of the hotel, hoping to catch a glimpse of the passersby's reactions. The ladies at the front desk smiled—they always do—and a diminutive white woman with large lips nodded approvingly.

Shit! Was that Angelina Jolie?

Ritz was looking and feeling like a million bucks as the doorman tipped his hat and motioned for her car. Her cab? Her hideous lime-green-and-yellow Crown Victoria. The cabdriver was smoking a stogie and was excited to let Ritz in his cab.

Ritz turned to the doorman and shook her head. "No. I'm sorry. Absolutely not. I called for a car service."

The driver was hurt, but not hampered. "Lauren Bacall got in my cab once. All the stars ride with Omar!"

The blond doorman tried hard not to laugh. "Ma'am, where are you headed, exactly?"

"To the Big Four headquarters, I have a pitch meeting. I can't roll up to my meeting in no green jitney."

"Hey, I'm not jiggy!" Omar joked. "Why you think Omar's cab no good? Come on, you're the African Queen, let Omar take you safely."

A short Italian man exited the hotel and a black sedan pulled up. The blond doorman opened the car door and sent them off.

Ritz was furious. "I want that car," she fumed. "That's the car service I wanted."

"That's his private driver," the doorman said. "Where you're going is less than three miles away. You won't be in the cab for more than five minutes, tops. You really shouldn't arrive late to your meeting. And when you pull up, no one will see you, anyway."

"What's so bad about being with Omar?" the driver chided.

"Omar, put out the goddamn cigar and we can roll," she said. "I want to arrive fresh."

"Sure, no problem. No problem, my African Queen."

Ritz peered inside the cab: typical gray pleather seats, no ugly surprises, thank goodness! She folded her body and slid inside.

"Take her to the Big Four headquarters, 4000 Wilshire Boulevard," the doorman said, closing her door. "And you knock 'em dead, ma'am, I'd love to hear all about it."

Ritz smiled. *That white boy was kinda cute. Hmm.*

The lime-green-and-yellow cab breezed down the street, only to come to a practical standstill. Traffic. Omar and his cab still reeked of cigars. Ritz was furious. What was supposed to be a five-minute ride was going to take considerably longer.

Wilshire Boulevard was the brain center for those

who worked behind the scenes in Hollywood, and it was always a mad dash to get to either side of it. So, it took twenty minutes to go three miles. And Omar's friendly-cabdriver routine was getting stale. Omar thought he was schooling her during the entire drive. When he was not speaking about politics and world events, he was making terrible jokes.

"You are lucky that you don't need the I-405. They call it the 405 because it takes four or five hours to maneuver!" Omar laughed.

Ritz wanted to scream. She had never met a living, breathing stereotype before. Omar was the star of his own minimovie, typecast as the funky cabdriver with the bad breath and the lame jokes. He was the joke!

The cab finally arrived. Omar screeched to a stop in front of the building. Ritz threw a $20 bill at him and exited the cab before Omar made a big production of opening her door for her. The last thing Ritz wanted was to be seen getting out of this cab.

Omar asked Ritz if she wanted her change.

"No!" she huffed, as she rushed to get into the building.

He threw the cab in drive and pushed on.

Ritz paused before entering the building. She wanted the breeze to hit her and knock some of that cab funk off her. A pack of tourists, about fifteen or so, stopped at the building's entrance. Their handlers were obviously keeping them on a tight leash. They marveled at the building, forcing Ritz to take a longer look. She had a few minutes to take in the site. She had planned to get here super-early to do a little reconnaissance. She didn't have time for that, but she did have a little time to appreciate her surroundings.

The Big Four headquarters was housed inside a beautiful neo-Gothic, thirty-eight-story building. Distinctive with its glazed, sparkling white terra-cotta tiles, the structure had two towers—east and west—connected by an open bridge at street level. The clock tower's plaque read that the building was completed in 1925 and became home to the Big Four eighty years later. The edifice was mesmerizing.

The tour guide's shrill voice snapped Ritz back to reality. "Let's move along, people, we have lots to see."

The lobby was slate gray and slick. Everything was marble or steel. The only color splash was the clump of network logos on display. Some logos were bigger than others, some were brighter. But somehow, there was a unified message: We are the Big Four. We are a team.

The tour guide stopped at the security desk, flashed a badge, and hustled the group along.

"The studios have collaborated to bring you great displays," he said. "First we're going to the wardrobe department, and later we'll visit the special effects display."

An older husband-and-wife pair lagged behind the tour group long enough to ask Ritz to take a picture.

"Sure," she said, delighted to be recognized.

Ritz placed her arm around the wife and smiled broadly for the husband. "So, where are you guys from?"

"Iowa," the husband huffed, while firmly placing the camera in Ritz's hand. "I asked you to take a picture of me and my wife in front of the logos."

"O-oh." Ritz tried to play it off. "Not a problem. Say cheese."

Just as she snapped, the eagle-eyed tour guide doubled back.

"Come along, folks," he said.

The husband snatched the camera and thanked Ritz weakly. The wife mumbled to him, "Who would jump into a stranger's vacation photo like that? These Angelinos are insane."

The short, Puerto Rican security guard zeroed in on Ritz. She had an attitude and asked, "May I help you?"

"Yes, I have an eleven a.m. appointment with Meredith," Ritz said, trying to ignore the attitude the guard was exuding.

"If you're here with NAG, usually y'all come in on Wednesdays. Are you sure you're scheduled for today?"

Ritz handed the guard her schedule. She scanned it and her telltale face said it all. She was impressed. And the funky attitude disappeared. The guard keyed the information into her tabletop keyboard. Ritz noticed her hot-pink fingernails, which were dazzling.

"You look familiar."

"Really?" Ritz responded. No need to flush that out, there'd been too much negative press lately. "I get that a lot."

The guard handed Ritz a badge. "You don't have to put it on. Just flash it if someone asks for it. The sticky tape never gets out of your clothes."

"Thank you for that."

"Sure. Please have a seat. I'll let them know that you're here."

The futuristic steel chair was as uncomfortable as it looked. Ritz cooled her heels for about ten minutes, then a striking, fortysomething black man approached. He was short, bald, with roundish glasses in front of the most gorgeous set of eyes Ritz had ever seen.

"Hi, we're ready for you now," he said in a rich baritone.

Ritz smiled to herself. *What? No Jennifers!* Once on the elevator, Ritz asked a few questions to break the ice.

"So, how long have you been here?" she said cheerfully.

"It feels like *too long* sometimes," he sighed.

The elevator trip was short, just to the second floor. When the doors opened, the man walked quickly around the corner as if to get away from her. He walked in front of her and led her to a conference room.

"Please meet Ritz Harper," he said to the others, almost as if he were an android.

The room was small, with a white marker board that was scribbled on, and a big glass table with four chairs. The network folks were sitting at the opposite end of the table. The three of them, the black guy, the white girl, and the white guy, huddled together like blades of grass. Ritz was alone at the other end, like the mushroom.

Clearly, the white guy was the leader of the pack. His name was Adam.

Adam Renfro was tall, with a healthy olive complexion and short brown hair. He was a modern James Dean, and the second attractive white guy that Ritz had bumped into today.

"Ritz Harper," Adam announced as he reached for Ritz's hand. "I'm happy to see that you had the fortitude to stop by, given the recent events."

He pulled out a chair for Ritz.

For Ritz, the meeting was starting on the right note; people knew her.

"What do you mean?" she asked.

"Your producer's attack, and the suicide, it's all over the news," Adam said.

"Oh, wow. Yeah, that *was* something." Ritz was stunned that the other media outlets had picked up the hot gossip. "That has really disturbed me, but not enough to stop the show."

Adam smiled. "That's the spirit. Let me introduce you to the others, this is Taha . . ."

The petite, black guy nodded.

Adam continued, "And this is Piper."

The youngish white girl briefly smiled. She was wearing stylish wide-rimmed glasses and a tight blouse.

But for now, they were the Jennifers to Ritz.

"Welcome, Ms. Harper," Piper spoke first. "This is a general, or a meet and greet. We must stress that many NAG members think that what Ian has given them is a contract to produce a show. Actually, what Ian gives you is a form that states you are entitled to a First Look Deal."

"I think mine is a little different," Ritz added.

Adam assured Ritz, "This is just preliminary ground rules that we must recite on behalf of the Big Four. We will definitely comb through your agreement at a later time. Not to worry."

"Thank you, Adam."

"Let me buzz in for a second," Taha said. "A First Look is just that, we get to meet you and see if what you're pitching is something we're interested in. So if this First Look goes well, and we think you have element . . ."

"*Element* is 'star power,' " said Piper. "It's the credibility to carry a project."

"Sure. Of course," Ritz said, taking it all in.

"Now, if we like your vision, we will green-light your project for production," Adam said. "Do you have any questions for us, Ritz?"

She smiled. "No, I understand. And I'm confident that you will like what I'm pitching."

Adam took the lead. "Great. So, Ritz, tell us about your television ambitions."

"Well, I want to host a talk show where I can discuss issues pertinent to our generation."

"Which generation is that?" Taha asked.

"Well, demographically, I am thinking about young urban professionals, the hip-hop community, grass-roots activists, progressive, hip whites, you know, the active audience members."

Adam placed his hand underneath his chin. "Generation Hot. We get it." He smiled. "So, you're looking at daytime talk, or nighttime?"

Ritz was stumped. She hadn't thought of that.

Piper said, "I'm thinking midafternoon, so definitely daytime, right, Ritz?"

Ritz nodded in agreement.

"Because nighttime would be more of an entertainment show, heavy on comedy and music," Taha added.

"Tell me specifically," Adam said slowly as if in deep thought, "what kind of topics would you like to cover on your talk show?"

"I would talk about everyday issues, hot news items, relationships, fashion, gossip, and celebrity-driven segments as well," Ritz said confidently.

"Your radio show put to television, right?" Piper asked. "That's an interesting concept."

"Absolutely," Ritz said. "But I wouldn't just want to film the radio show. I am going for originality in content for television. People tune in to radio and television for very different reasons. I want to make certain that the TV show is on target."

Adam and the others smiled politely, but with little enthusiasm.

The brief silence was deafening; Ritz wished Aaron was on the scene to liven things up with a sound effect.

Adam glanced at his watch and scribbled a few more notes. He rose and extended his hand. "It was very, very good to meet you. We're going to kick this around a little more and we'll be in touch."

Oh no, she thought. *It can't end this soon.*

"Do you think you really have a grasp of my concept?" Ritz stalled.

Piper extended her hand. "Oh, yeah, we get the gist. It's promising."

Taha smiled and nodded in agreement. He rose to shake Ritz's hand. Taha's handshake was weak and soft. She was hoping to feel a handshake that was a little more confident.

Ritz collected her purse.

"You know, that's a great blouse," Taha whispered. "Chanel, right?"

Ritz smiled. "Nothing is more endearing than a man who knows his fashion."

Taha leaned in close. "And a man who knows another man."

Ritz was startled. "What?"

"I mean the bow, the blouse, you're concealing an

Adam's apple, right? I mean, if you're a woman, you're beautiful, but if you're a guy-to-girl, well, that's *really* hot."

"Taha, I'm a woman. And I'm insulted!"

He was apologetic. "I am so sorry. This is Hollywood . . . you never know what's going on underneath other people's clothes. Please forgive me, it was meant to be a compliment."

With that, Ritz thanked the executives and exited the room. She pulled the door behind her and lingered long enough to hear the chatter.

"I think this breaking news has her Q rating all over the map, but when this dies down, I don't see anything promising," Adam said.

"But you know what?" Taha said excitedly. "I'm thinking that's a great format for Paris Hilton, or Lindsay Lohan."

"Oh my gosh, yes!" yelled Piper. "But we'd have to get one of them on the radio first."

"So, do we have to do anything more with her? She is from Ian—"

"No," Taha said. "Just meeting with her satisfies the affirmative action quota. On that note, I'm black, and don't hate me for saying this, but this affirmative action program has run its course. I mean, come on. Why do you need a diversity program for Hollywood? You need a leg up for Hollywood? That's an insult.

"Halle, Jamie, Denzel, Forest Whitaker, Morgan Freeman, Whoopi, hell, even Jennifer Hudson has an Oscar. I mean *jeez!*"

Ritz's hands were shaking. *Those fucking Jennifers.* She was tapping her foot. *Don't cry, girl. Don't cry. Hold it together.*

Hearing Taha, the lone *brother,* repitching her show idea with white actresses and then attacking affirmative action was the last straw to cap off a long weekend of disappointments. She headed to the elevator.

Tears pooled in Ritz's eyes. She felt the sting of mascara. If she blinked, the tears would fall. *Do not blink, girl. Do not blink!* She didn't have to blink. The tears began to fall uncontrollably. She put on her sunglasses.

The elevator doors opened to reveal a very pregnant blonde with a network badge dangling from her neck. She exited the elevator but paused and smiled at Ritz.

"Hey, what are you doing on this floor?" the blonde asked Ritz.

Ritz entered the elevator and returned the smile. "Nothing much."

The elevator door closed. The blonde turned the corner and caught Piper, Taha, and Adam leaving the pitch room.

"Oh no, the fuck you didn't!" she yelled.

"What, Meredith?" Piper questioned.

"Don't you 'what' me!" Meredith said. "You just signed Ritz Harper and a FOX rep wasn't at the meeting?"

"What did you say?"

"I said I'm calling Rutger. You motherfuckers signed Ritz Harper, the Queen of Radio, behind my fucking back? What do you think, I'm stupid? You think I'm out of commission because I'm pregnant!"

"Holy shit!" Adam said, turning red. "I thought we just had to meet her to make the AA quota."

"Make the quota? That woman has been on every station around the clock," Meredith said. "She is the biggest fucking story since the presidential election. Have you lost your minds!"

"Meredith, she came through Ian. We thought it was one of the NAG generals," Piper explained.

"Really? Just a general? And Ian sends her on a fucking Monday? Give me the paperwork."

Meredith scanned it, then held it up to Piper's face. "Those big-ass glasses and you still can't read? Ritz Harper was supposed to be in a green-light meeting with me and my team, not a First Look with you basement morons. It's right here, Piper, in bold. Rutger will hear about this insubordination in sixty seconds. And if I were you, I'd start pitching my résumé!"

The angry pregnant blonde waddled off leaving a trail of expletives behind her.

28

Too WHOT to Handle

Ernest Ruffin, aka Ruff, was the station manager for WHOT, and for the past twenty years the single force keeping the radio station together. But in this new age of technology and instant celebrity, Ruff's rapid transformation from a top-level management hotshot to an aging tortoise had made him bitter and desperate for the golden days of radio. Ruff managed people, forecasted industry trends, and never allowed himself to get caught up in the shady side of working in radio. Until now.

The old-school radio legend unleashed every trick

in the book to dethrone Ritz Harper. With an army consisting of journalist Michelle Davis, Abigail Gogel, Chas James sympathizers, and a city of disgruntled *Ritz Harper Excursion* folks behind him, the Queen of Radio was scheduled to be out of a job in less than twenty-four hours.

Ruff had all the bases covered, save one: the Spiritual Tsunami, Tracee Remington (soon to be) Jordan.

29

Ritz hated airport terminals because they were filthy, and LAX was the worst. Well, not the worst, but when you despise germs, and especially untraceable, contagious, international germs, LAX was the worst.

So Ritz sat in her public seat trying desperately not to eat or drink anything that would force her to use the public toilet. She'd rather go on the plane, where there was an element of cleanliness, at least between flights.

Flight 924 had a connection at Washington Dulles International Airport, before landing at Newark Liberty International Airport in New Jersey. Factor in the time change, and Ritz wouldn't make it home until midnight.

That would be cool, except for the circumstances behind the travel. This upcoming meeting with the Three Suits scheduled for early Tuesday couldn't be good. Still, Ritz was surprisingly in a good mood. While her pitch meeting had turned into a disaster, she'd managed to pull it together and was proud of the way she'd handled herself with grace and dignity in the midst of the storm. And she wasn't going to give up. If anything, those Three Stooges, aka the Jennifers, made her want to prove them wrong. She wasn't going anywhere. *They will see me again,* she thought. *And when they do, they'll be sorry.*

Ritz was going back to New York. She was going to reclaim her throne and make everything right in radio land, have a couple of off-the-chart ratings books, and watch the TV people come for her. Yes, she would probably be needing a new producer, but Ritz was ready to face that challenge, too. She decided she would take Tracee's advice and start planting her Go-Getter garden.

Ruff was ready, too. He had been planning his attack. He had been meeting with his army, making sure they all had their marching orders and were ready to do their particular parts. He was fighting this war against

Ritz Harper on many fronts. He knew it would not be easy to derail the *Ritz Harper Excursion*. But that's why plans were necessary. This could not be an overnight venture. It was years in the making. A few days after Ritz was shot, Ruff had pulled Chas's coat about his plan. He told Ritz's producer that while WHOT was number one in the afternoon drive-time ratings, it wasn't secure in that spot. It was only bolstered by the shooting, which had people tuning in, the way folks hold up traffic rubbernecking after an accident. The ratings weren't real. And before the shooting, Ritz was on the decline.

But he had an answer that would shake up the industry—FOX News reporter Michelle Davis.

Michelle, the honey-baked, early-thirtysomething newswoman, landed the gig as Ritz Harper's seat-filler, and Ruff's plans were firmly in motion.

When it came to crossover, Michelle had all the bases covered. Men loved Michelle because she spun old-school R&B, blended with blue-eyed soul, and she was a sports fanatic. Michelle had carved a niche for herself, the "Between the Beats" segment, where she interviewed music and sports stars during the drive. Not the typical studio shock-jock antics, either; Michelle knew how to interview. She would gently coax the subjects into breaking news on her show. She was a journalist.

The women loved Michelle because she gossiped and kept it real about her own drama. In her "Don't

Mess with Him, Girl" segment, women could call in and blast out some man who had done them wrong. Women could keep it going on the Web site that Michelle had created that had the names of these creeps, their offense, and their pictures because she didn't want any other sister getting played out.

Michelle played the educated-corporate-hottie role to the hilt and stayed on the streets mixing it up with her listeners. And her voice—Michelle purred with an intoxicating blend of the Queen's English and ride-or-die bitch prose when she was on her soapbox. During her time warming Ritz's seat, she caught fire. Michelle's ratings bested the best of Ritz's. That was all Ruff needed to see. He was sold. Ritz had to go.

Ritz was still number one, but her act was growing stale. People were onto her, and she had to play cat and mouse to get stars to fess up. And if stars didn't give up the dirt, Ritz would blast them and kick them out of the studio. It made for good Internet buzz, but how long would this format last?

In the beginning, Chas worked diligently to keep Michelle out of Ritz's seat and away from her time slot. But when Ruff explained why Ritz was going down and taking the station with her, Chas knew, too, that he had to come up with another game plan.

Ruff and Chas were having coffee, going over the trades and reeling at how the fans were forcing the music industry and the radio industry to morph into the land of the open source.

"Look at the landscape," Ruff said to Chas. "The artists and the listeners are learning to collaborate without the radio and record-label middlemen. The artists release new music directly to the fans. The fans control and promote the content by downloading the songs, creating their own playlists and blasting the music everywhere. The artists are keeping more of their money. The listeners are hearing the music before we get it. The blueprint of radio doesn't necessarily include us anymore. And the iPod has all but killed us!"

Chas nodded. He knew Ruff was right.

"The format, as we know it now, isn't stable for us," Ruff continued, referring to people such as him and Chas. "Personalities will have their parachute, always. But you and me, not so much."

"So what are you saying?" Chas stammered.

"Having the hottest show in New York, and securing syndication in other markets, that's good for Ritz, but it's not for you. She's complacent, and she's sabotaging her career. Her sabotaged career is your murdered career."

Ruff had more, much more, to say. Every coffee break with Ruff was purposeful; he didn't believe in wasting conversation.

"And Ritz has no right to be complacent right now," Ruff said. "*Billboard* published an item about Michelle's ratings inching into Ritz's territory. Abigail is a little too happy about that."

But Ruff shared an even more ominous vision:

"You know, *urban* doesn't mean 'black,' and *black* doesn't mean 'hip-hop,' and the whole format is shifting. Look around. There's an imminent whitening of all the urban stations. The first phase is to buy the black radio-station owners out. The Three Suits have done that already. Abigail doesn't own shit but her last name. We know this.

"The second phase is to take the strongest black voices off the air and replace them with commercial, more palatable white and brown voices. The third phase—which the Three Suits are actually fighting—is to manipulate the urban ratings. The long view is that we're all about to get jacked."

Chas was bewildered and scared. "What would be the purpose of fucking with the ratings? We're making money for the Three Suits. And the urban shows are capturing the crossover market; most of them are younger listeners, who stream the shows on the Web. And that's good for us, you know, that broadens the listening base, increases our ratings. So how could they jack us?"

Ruff grabbed a napkin and wiped the sleep out of his eyes. This phase haunted him the most.

"This business goes through cycles where it just cannibalizes itself," he replied. "It's a shady business. SoundTron invented these personal electronic radio monitors that report who listens to what in real time. The old ratings measuring method, where people reported what they listened to in their diaries, is gone.

The diaries were fairer to urban formats and, in some instances, helped our ratings. But now SoundTron's electronic monitors are skewed against urban radio stations from the jump because very few urban listeners are carrying the damn things around! More whites have them, and when they're at home, in the car, or even if they walk into a store and the lite FM shit is playing in the background, that station is clocked and gets a boost in the ratings.

"No one is clocking what the urban listeners are listening to, and when the SoundTron report is released next month, our ratings will drop. When the ratings drop, the advertising rates drop, too. The advertisers are in bed with SoundTron. They have been waiting for a measuring tool to justify lower rates and paying us less money. Urban stations across the board will lose money. Every station will be fighting for national syndication in major markets. Ultimately, those shows that are syndicated will put a locally produced show—even if it's high in ratings—out of work. You are in thirty markets but not the big markets. And you can kiss your show good-bye."

Chas was speechless. He could see it all happening right before his eyes. His whole star was hitched to this radio game and, for the longest time, to Ritz Harper. But what Ruff was saying made him have to reevaluate because Chas wasn't about to let his star fade.

"The perfect storm of shady advertisers, greedy suits, and covert ratings manipulation has sounded the death knell for urban formats," Ruff added as the final piece of punctuation.

"What can save us?" Chas asked.

"When everything is the same, the different thing thrives. Hot, celebrity-fueled escapism, as always," Ruff blurted. "Fused with sex appeal and intelligent talk. No one is doing that right now but Michelle Davis. That's why her ratings are through the roof. Studio drama is good. Fan devotion is better. She's building that. And that's the kind of loyalty that keeps you in business."

30

Ritz Harper exited the plane with her hair pulled back into a long ponytail. She was wearing concealer, lip gloss, and wide-rimmed Moss Lipow shades. Ritz wasn't the woman in red, she wasn't the impeccable, impestuous diva, she wasn't the Queen of Radio. She was complex: equal parts renewed, confused, and hopeful.

After that stint in "Hell-Ay," the old Ritz would have huddled in a dark corner and smoked a joint. She had the urge to score back when she was packing to leave Los Angeles. So she slipped on her antidrug shield—a throwback, white T-shirt with KDC embla-

zoned on the front in bold, red letters. No one knew
what KDC stood for, not even Chas and Tracee, and
that was the point. Ritz didn't want to spark a fashion
frenzy, she wanted a personal reminder for herself and
to herself about what happens when talented people
do drugs.

The dressed-down Ritz resembled a caramel, six-
foot Jackie O as she strolled to luggage claim. Usually
Chas handled this part for her, but these days she was
flying solo. Ritz was so awash in random thoughts that
she didn't notice the growing commotion behind her.

"Ritz Harper! Hey, everybody, the Queen is back!"

Ritz hesitated before she turned around. The last
time a stranger called her name he shot her.

"Ritz, we love you!" said one woman. "Ritz! Over
here, Ritz!"

Ritz smiled, gushed, laughed, and waved. The
more they screamed, the more she loved them back.
The crowd was growing larger and a motley crew
of Transportation Security Administration officials
(TSA)—an elderly white man, two youngish black
guys, and a tall Hispanic guy—circled her and escorted her to baggage claim.

The fans surrounded baggage claim, cheek to
cheek, and at least six bodies deep. Camera phones
and flashing lights blinded her. She heard the love,
but she wanted to feel it, too.

Ritz demanded that the TSA back off. "Those are
my people!" she exclaimed. "Let me see my people!
Long live the Queen, baby!"

TSA eased up just a bit and allowed Ritz to plant herself by the conveyer belt and take photos with her fans. After well over an hour, the crowd still hadn't eased up. By this time, the media were there. From CNN to BBC. *Who told them?*

A mic was shoved in her face; at the other end was news reporter Michelle Davis. Ritz gave her a strong hug and whispered in her ear, "Thank you so much for representing. I heard you really raised the bar."

Michelle was puzzled by that. She was also livid that her producer at FOX had made her cover her competition.

"We're glad you're back, Ritz Harper," said Michelle, pretending to really care. "Now that you're leaving the radio station, what will you do next?"

"Leaving?" Ritz said in shock on camera. "I'm not leaving. Baby, I'm glad to be back!"

With that, the crowd roared in applause.

Above the noise, and the instant paparazzi, Ritz heard her Tracee: *"Ritgina Harper. Get down from there!"*

Ritz craned her neck to see Tracee, looking the part of a feisty Penny today.

"This is my best friend, Tray, everybody!" squealed Ritz.

More photos, more love. TSA handled Ritz's bags, and Tracee handled Ritz. Finally, they made it to the car, where Randolph was waiting.

Tracee was still fussing as the TSA brought Ritz's bags to the car. "I have to find out from the news that

you're home! Your security is at risk and you're sign-
ing autographs? Ritzy, what were you thinking!"

The TSA, lingering to get her autograph for themselves, laughed at that. Randolph, seeing the situation,
asked if any of them had a camera. They all did. Ritz
smiled and hammed it up for her impromptu security
team. She was genuinely happy. Her huge smile
reached her eyes and then some.

"I can't believe you are out here taking pictures in
your Kurt Cobain T-shirt!" Tracee teased her.

The color rushed from Ritz's face. "How did you
know—this is my special shirt!"

"KDC is famous," said one of the young TSA
agents. "That's Kurt Donald Cobain. Those initials are
as famous as KFC!"

The older white TSA guy chimed in, "I made a Jimi
Hendrix shirt for my granddaughter who parties a lot
at the University of Wisconsin."

"Ritz has a Bob Marley and a Billie Holiday shirt,
too," Tracee told the guy. "She'd never tell a soul, but
Ritz has a love affair with grunge music. She can never
get enough of Nirvana."

Everyone laughed. And Ritz, who was feeling as if
she couldn't have any more damn secrets, had to
laugh, too.

Tracee stood next to Randolph and he hugged
her closer. Ritz did a double take. This was the first
time that she had ever seen her brother and her best
friend side by side. Morris Chestnut and Janet "Penny"

Jackson—and they were glowing. Not that cheap-ass after-sex glow, but something deeper, something pure. They were in love.

"And what have you two been up to? When did you flee that retirement village?"

Tracee flashed her ring. "Randolph proposed last night. We're kidnapping you later. We're all going out to dinner."

BAM! SMACK! KAPOW! Ritz's ego suffered the death blow.

The night she met the Morris Chestnut look-alike—and before she discovered that he was her half brother—Randolph refused to sleep with her! He was saving himself for "wife material." Randolph must have found it. Ritz could never compete with plain-Jane Tracee in the wifey category. *The Bible-thumpers always get the ring; the deejays always get the married men.*

"Ritzy, baby, we're going to be sisters!" Tracee cooed.

"We have always been sisters, right?" said Ritz. "You didn't have to find my long-lost brother to make it legit!"

The TSA officers returned to the terminal. One shouted back, "Ms. Remington, thank you for the e-mail. I've been wanting to meet her for a long time!"

Ritz looked at Tracee. "What e-mail?"

"I know this business. Some people must stage an event for publicity, others just arrive. I sent a few social-media blitzes that you were due to arrive. But all of these people interrupted their lives to come see you, in the wee hours of the morning! I had to make sure WHOT didn't forget who you are."

"And having Michelle interview me?"

"Yeah, that was bad of me. That's why I have to stay in my Bible. I know how bad I can be."

Randolph initiated the group hug with his two women—the one woman he was destined to find, which led him to the one woman he was destined to love.

"Now that's a picture!" said an onlooker. "I'll shoot it for you. On three. *Uno. Dos. Tres . . .* "

FLASH.

Randolph leaned over and planted a big kiss on Ritz's forehead. "Welcome home, Sis," he said, feeling that he might actually get used to having Ritz as his sister.

"This is so strange, Tracee."

"How do you mean?"

"One minute, I'm known and pretty famous, the next minute I'm treated like a nobody. I go to Los Angeles and get treated like a peon."

"So things didn't go well at the pitch meeting, huh?"

"Shit!" Ritz slipped out. "They clowned me. For real."

Tracee smiled slyly. "So you know that you just confessed to going to the pitch meeting after you promised to skip it."

"Damn! That's right." Even Ritz had to laugh about it.

"Not that you could keep a secret from me," Tracee reminded her. "A colleague of mine called. She saw you at the Big Four."

"See what I mean, Tray? The fools that I was pitching to didn't care who I was or what I had to say. I was wasting their time and they made sure that I knew it."

"There are beggars and choosers in Hollywood, and everywhere else in the world. The lesson from meeting with Rutger and the others is that you've got to know who you are and you've got to recognize your own status," Tracee said. "If you walk in the door begging for a big break, you will be played like a beggar. You will be told that you're nothing; or that it's nothing they can do for you without calling in a special favor—that's the game. They break you down—in order to make you believe that you need their services— because once you need them, they can demand things from you."

Randolph was nodding in agreement and couldn't help but add his two cents. "And if you roll with a whore, you'll be played like a whore."

"What?" Ritz thought that came out of left field. "What are you talking about?"

"I told him everything that happened," Tracee said.

"I hope I'm not overstepping," Randolph tried to explain. "But from what I understand, Rutger always

viewed Chas as a sex partner, or his candy. If Chas introduced you, they can't help but view you in the same
way, as an extra piece of candy. Chas could have never
brought you to the place you needed to be because of
how he came to the game. So you were set up to fail."

And he's wise, too! Ritz smiled to herself at this reve-
lation. Randolph was absolutely right. But she was also
concerned because she could no longer speak to her
friend without knowing that she would also be sharing
her business with Randolph, too. That annoyed her a
bit. But she wasn't going to ruin the moment by letting
Tracee know this. Not quite yet.

"You've worked hard for this, people have invested
in you because they see your worth," Tracee said. "You
never have to beg for what is rightfully yours."

31

How You Doin'?

The Three Suits—the tanned and toned suit from the Culver City, California, office; the grumpy gray suit from the Chicago office; and the cowboy-hat-wearing suit from the Dallas office—called an emergency meeting with the entire WHOT staff, including Ritz Harper.

The last time the Three Suits had made an appearance was to announce they were the new owners of the station. From that point, the Three Suits existed only as signatures on WHOT internal memos, bonus checks, and holiday cards. So whatever brought them to New York had to be big.

The California suit was the only one who spoke.

"As we all know, we made headlines because of a damning incident involving producer Chas James, and a disgruntled rap artist who had apparently stalked Ritz Harper."

Ruff and Abigail traded glances. At last the shoe was going to drop on Ritz's big head! The ratings-hungry beast would no longer be WHOT's albatross.

"We've invited FOX News reporter Michelle Davis to join us to shed some light on why we're here," the California suit said. "Well, let's get to it, shall we? How did the entire world learn about Chas's unfortunate incident? Can you help us with that Ms. Harper?"

Ritz treaded lightly. "I called the studio hotline."

"And what happened next?"

Tony cleared his throat before responding. "I punched the call through to Michelle. At the time, I didn't know what Ritz was going to say, she just said that she had breaking news."

"I asked Ritz if Chas was okay," Michelle butted in. "Really, I was mortified that she would be so callous as to discuss his rape on air."

Rumblings fell over the room.

"I ran from my office," Ruff cut in. "I felt that call was damaging to our station and I had to put an end to it."

"And, Mr. Ruffin, what do you think of this whole scenario? Put it in perspective for us and tell us what should happen next."

"Ritz lowered the boom on quality radio programming. She's ruthless and ratings-driven, even when it comes to a producer who slaves for her. For years, we've all worked as a team to support the *Excursion,* and she goes and plays one of us like that? I think we all can agree that Ritz Harper should be terminated. Immediately."

"Mr. Ruffin speaks for me," Abigail said. "As a woman, I can imagine how devastating rape must be, and I am very, very disappointed in Ritz. Very."

Ritz remained silent. But she made a mental note of who was throwing daggers at her back and stabbing her right in the chest.

"We're not going to discuss personal ethics," Jamie said, getting involved. "But as an on-air personality, she did the right thing. She broke the story first. The story involved her, but it was bigger than her. She was brave to do it."

"What are you smoking, Jamie?" Abigail argued. "What's brave about Ritz poking fun at a rape victim who was trying to save her life? And you, you of all people should know how destructive that woman is."

"The word on the street and on all the other stations is that Ritz was in danger and that Chas hooked up with the dude anyway," Jamie said. "Ask Aaron about how many calls he dropped or screened out when the callers tried to tell Michelle the truth. Better yet, why didn't Chas talk about it? He loves the spotlight. Why did he lay low and then retire?"

"The word on the street doesn't mean shit," Ruff growled.

"It does in radio," the California suit said. "The word on the street is our lifeline."

Ritz stared at Ruff and Abigail. Ruff was a radio relic, now mad at the new generation. Of course he would bond with Michelle Davis, a newsperson who had wet dreams about producing edutainment from her own soapbox. And Abigail was a powerless figurehead, without the figure. They weren't friends; they'd always plotted against her, but now they're brazen about it.

Ritz looked at Jamie, and Jamie rolled her eyes, for the first time showing her true feelings for Ritz. Ritz scoped Aaron; his head was so far up Michelle Davis's ass nowadays that he didn't return her glance. Aaron's loyalty had always wavered a little too much for Ritz's taste, anyhow.

Chas had thrown the biggest dagger of all. The rape would have devastated Ritz had she not known the real deal behind the incident, thanks to detectives Pelov and Maddow. The only person who got a pass from Ritz was Jamie. Ritz realized that Jamie was just an ambitious young woman, but she was honest and forthright and in the end would always do the right thing.

Ritz had learned a few things in Hollywood, and one was that she had to change.

Ritz made a silent and personal vow to atone to

Jamie. She would begin by steering clear of Derek. (Where in the hell was he, anyway?) And, most important, laying a foundation for the young associate producer to blaze her own trail.

"After hearing these sentiments, Ms. Harper, tell us, if you had the opportunity to do it all over again, would you make that call?"

"*Yes,*" Ritz said adamantly. "If given the opportunity to break the story or hold it, I would break it all over again. This is a business. This is *show* business. No one in this room took a vow of silence with the media when I was shot and was left for dead. In fact, Chas sent a press release. Thus, my loyalty is to the listeners."

The suits clapped excitedly.

"Yes, Ms. Harper, you are right!" the California suit said. "Ritz Harper is our future. She is the future of radio. She gets it. She gets why we are here. Ritz's call was played all around the world, and we hit record ratings never before seen in the history of radio! That one phone call took us to a global audience. The only problem, which brought us here today, is that there was no video to accompany Ritz's call. And that's why we're collaborating with the Big Four networks to give the Queen of Radio her own daytime television talk show!"

Ritz was stunned silent.

The Chicago suit finally spoke.

"Those of you who were so appalled by Ritz's actions, you may want to reevaluate why you're here and why we're in the business. Ritz, Meredith at FOX, she's on maternity leave now, has signed the most fabulous multitalented television-show producer for you, and we are very confident that you will work well together. Let's all welcome the executive producer of the new *Ritz Harper Excursion* television show, Tracee Remington!"

Ritz could not believe her ears. She was afraid to turn around because she wanted to contain her excitement, which was impossible.

Tracee smiled and kept a professional demeanor. She was wearing her best blue pinstripe suit. She hadn't had on a suit in years and she was surprised it still fit. Tracee was glad to be back from retirement and asserted her power: "Everyone in this room is entitled to a fresh start. I am excited and looking forward to working with each of you. And over the next few days, I will introduce you to our television production team.

"Let me be clear: you're either with the *Ritz Harper Excursion* or you're out of here. And that's not a threat: it's a guarantee. However, for those of you who wish to join us on our television set, you are clearly welcome to do so. We need the extra hands and your great ideas."

32

Tuesday, 7:45 p.m.
Short Hills, New Jersey
Hilton Twilight Spa
Spa reception area

For Ritz and Tracee, the after-work spa retreat was a welcomed stress buster that recalled fond memories.

The Hilton spa was a favorite urban retreat for Ritz and Tracee in the days before Tracee retired and relocated to Florida. The location was great because it was close to Ritz's home and offered privacy; the well-heeled clientele never tripped on Ritz's celebrity. Now that the spa had twilight hours, the friends could visit as often as needed.

"You know I don't like planned activities, but we will conduct our work-related business at the office, and our *Sistah Girl* friendship business here," Tracee announced. "Is that cool with you?"

"Of course," Ritz said. "Let's get down to the sistah girl biz, then. Once upon a time, you told me that we were friends because we were wise enough to never work together. So what's up with our new work relationship?"

The spa attendant approached to offer cool refreshments. The ladies each took a glass of purified water with mint leaves.

Tracee smiled. "The more Randolph and I talked, the more we realized that you're my assignment. I could either walk away from you, or do what God wants me to do, and that is to be your friend and your sister." Tracee flashed her engagement ring. "Your real sister!"

"Speaking of my new cocounsel," Ritz zinged, "are you going to tell all of my business to my brother? Because if so, we're going to have some issues."

"Ritzy, I was scared of who you were becoming," Tracee said between sips. "Honestly, I didn't know how low you would go. I talked to Randolph about your trials in L.A. because I was so fearful of all what was going down. He's so wise, and I didn't think before I spoke. But I will from now on. Trust me, your listening party is still a party of one."

"You put my shit in the vault."

"That's right," Tracee said. "Never to be unsealed."

"What do you mean, you were scared of *who* I was becoming? Damn, Tray. Ouch."

Tracee politely conceded that she was harsh.

"Here's what I mean," she said, trying to clean it up. "It's good to be driven; it's dangerous to be too driven. Your measure of success is ratings. And when you see ratings at the finish line, nothing else matters."

Ritz took a sip and swallowed hard. "I think that is the mark of a successful person. If I make pit stops along the way or if I think too hard or too long, someone else can just swoop in and take it from me."

"Take *what* from you, Ritzy?"

"My success. My name, my throne, my audience, my show, my ratings, my money, and my life. They just want to take it all. Tray, there are people who smile in my face every day and they secretly want me out of their way. It's numbing sometimes. Everybody has an angle. Look at what Chas did; and everybody does it."

Tracee threw up her hand in disagreement. "I'm not claiming that. There are rules and laws that we must follow in every walk, and if you sit back and be fearful about who wants to take something from you, well, baby, they've already won. See, here's the thing. What is for you is yours alone, and nobody can take it. No matter how hard they try."

"I don't think you understand, so let me break it down for you. My own producer handed me over to the man who tried to kill me. He did that. Now, how does your theory work in that scenario?"

"Ritzy, I'm glad you asked. When you think about what Chas did, you zero in on his intent. I zero in on the outcome. Chas wanted you out of his way, and because what is for you is yours alone, he was removed."

Ritz hadn't thought of it that way.

"And," Tracee continued, "when Hardcore wanted you dead, because what is for you is yours alone, he's no longer here."

That was a fact and Ritz knew it.

"And," Tracee couldn't stop now, "you had three little haters biting at your back, Michelle Davis, Abigail, and Ruff. They collaborated to publicly humiliate you, and kick you off your throne. Now, tell me what happened to them?"

Ritz didn't need to say a word. Michelle Davis was so sure of taking over Ritz's show that she'd reduced her hours at FOX. Now someone was in her prime position at FOX, and she had been relegated to fill-in duties for the *V Spot*. Abigail and Ruff had made it known in front of the owners that they had no idea how to handle the radio station in an ever-changing climate. Especially Abigail.

I never thought I'd hear someone say that the word on the street didn't matter, Ritz thought.

Tracee interrupted Ritz's private reflections. "It's not hocus-pocus, Ritz. It's karma. If you respect karma, it will protect you. And it works both ways. So now, you must do right by Jamie to put your karma on the right path."

"What? You're tripping, Tray. Jamie will be fine."

Tracee was serious. "As your executive producer, I am firmly suggesting that you give Jamie her job back on the *Ritz Harper Excursion* . . . and you treat her well."

Ritz nearly dropped her drink. "Not after what Chas did, no more stray dogs," Ritz protested. "I'll be nice to her, but that's it. She's a brat."

"That brat is the only person who had your back in the meeting with the Three Suits. Despite all that you've done, and all that she's tried to do, Jamie spoke up for you when the others were leading you to the gallows."

"I'm not kissing her ass, Tray."

"Fine, don't kiss her ass. Just let her do her thing."

"Not a problem. Not a problem at all."

"And—"

"Oh, hell nawl, ain't no more *and*s, Tray!" Ritz laughed. "That's it."

"And, give Jamie a space on your television show. Start her at the bottom and get out of her way and let her work her way up."

"No, she'll be hogging the camera. Absolutely not!"

"Ritz, be a woman of substance and stop playing bitch games. The more you do for others, the more that comes back to you. Use your voice, your mic, and your power to do a good deed every now and then, to deflect all that horrible gossip you spew!"

"You like my gossip."

"Yes, I do, and I reach for my Bible immediately thereafter."

"I appreciate what you're doing for me, Tray, and I'll work hard."

"I already know that. I appreciate you luring me

out of retirement. Now I realize that there's a thin line between resting and *resting in peace*."

The friends laughed.

Ritz took a sip. "Real talk. I want to see Derek again."

Tracee shook her head and laughed. "Of course you do. But for what?"

Ritz's eyes grew wide. "For conversation, I guess. I don't know. I know that I am not supposed to see him anymore. I've promised myself that I wouldn't hurt Jamie anymore by creeping with him. I don't want *that*. Maybe I do . . . but that and more. I know it's ridiculous. I mean, he's shorter than me, he's younger than me, he's shady . . ."

"You're shadier than him, though!" Tracee joked.

"I want your blessing on that, Tray. I like him."

Tracee watched her friend. "You're serious. *Wow*. I can't give you that blessing . . . that has to come from Jamie."

"I thought you would say that," Ritz huffed. "Do you think she'd give it to me?"

"Something tells me that Jamie is going to be so grateful for what you're doing for her, and she's going to be so busy building her career with the exciting opportunities that you're giving to her, that she won't have time to run behind Derek's yellow ass. That's a new-age career girl, honey. They don't sit around and cry in their Sapphire martinis like we used to. They've adapted to the game. They keep it moving!"